RETRIBUTION

3/2/19

Carmin –

I hope you enjoy my
story.

Thank you.

Evie

Evelyn L. Tankersley

RETRIBUTION

EVELYN L. TANKERSLEY

Published by: ELT Books

2413 Mourning Warbler Avenue

North Las Vegas, Nevada 89084

E-mail: eltbooks@peoplepc.com

Harley Davidson ™; Jeep ™

Cover Collage Photography by Conrad Basilio

Graphics by: Mustang Graphic Designers;
www.MustangGFX.com

MustangGraphic@aol.com

(916)599-4942

Story and characters are fiction.

DEDICATED TO ALL THOSE WHO HAVE BEEN:

SEXUALLY VIOLATED

MY SPECIAL THANKS GO TO:

MY PARENTS FOR GIVING ME A WONDERFUL CHILDHOOD AND EDUCATION

MY CHILDREN FOR ALWAYS BEING THERE FOR ME

AUTHOR NANCY L. CRATTY FOR CONSTANT ENCOURAGEMENT AND CONSTRUCTIVE CRITICISM

PROFESSOR KAREN MULCAHY FOR ETERNAL OBJECTIVITY

MARY ABEL AND ALLIE ANDERSEN FOR ALWAYS BEING WILLING TO READ MY MANUSCRIPTS

CONRAD BASILIO FOR CREATING A DISTINCTIVE BOOK COVER

RETRIBUTION

Evelyn L. Tankersley

The twelve foot wooden doors to the Tudor style mansion were open wide. The trunk of the body was still hanging by the duct taped feet on hooks with woven straps tied around the atrium staircase spindles. The head, penis, and neatly folded skin were beneath the open throat. Blood still oozed.

I

Cyanna had purposely not visited her father's grave since that day over a year ago when she had come to tell him that the men who butchered him were themselves butchered and by her own hand. She had come full circle, and she knew he would have understood and approved because he had taught her with their fishing trip so many years ago when the sturgeon was over length, that to legalize a being, it must have its head, tail, and skin removed. Somehow, she needed his closeness, because she

1

had just *murdered and made very legal another asshole that really needed killin'.*

"Daddy, I miss you so much!" Tears streamed down her cheeks. She knelt in front of his headstone and began blubbering about meeting her twin Lexi, and she didn't blame him for stealing her from her dying mother at birth, and maybe he didn't even know about the other baby. She said she loved Gram, and this asshole she had just legalized was responsible for her death. There was so much to tell him. She was choking and swallowed up in sobbing. She was soon in a fetal position in front of the stone, and the warm desert evening enveloped her with only a sliver of moonlight for protection.

***

The next morning, not far away from the rubble that was once their co-workers' home, the CSI team presence was evident on the mountainside at the residence of the recently mutilated mob lord.

Gus was on the scene in front of the charred fort. He was stricken; he loved Lexi and had for years, but always thought he was too old for her. To lose her now, when he was just getting the courage to approach her with the possibility of something more than friendship between them, left him the same color as his remaining hair. His skin was pallid, and his eyes were blood shot from unshed tears.

A shiny black sports car pulled up in front of the fort and stopped abruptly beside Gus. As the dust settled, the driver's door opened and a very tall, well dressed thirty-something man emerged. He had grabbed his jacket as he exited and was pulling it on as he approached Gus. Offering his hand, he said, "Eddie DeLuca, Chicago PD."

Gus was impressed by the fact that they could look one another in the eye. He knew Eddie must be at least 6'5". The ripple of the silk sleeve over his biceps as he slipped into his jacket indicated the well developed muscles underneath. He had rich black hair and matching eyes.

"You knew the people that lived here?" he asked as he noticed the strained look on his face.

"Lexi was CSI and an incredible young lady. We will all miss her," he said as he looked away.

"Do you think she perished in the fire?"

"We have just begun our investigation," he said as he nodded toward the smoldering embers. "You're a long way from home. Why would Chicago be interested in this business?"

"We are actually interested in the other one, that grisly murder in the castle up the mountain. But there were so many cars and people going in different directions, I couldn't get anyone's attention."

"That's part of the reason I'm here by myself. They need everyone up there. Gus Ferguson is my name," he said as he flashed his badge to the officer who reciprocated.

"Gus, can you tell me anything about the murder up the hill?"

"All we know is what was reported originally. We had a very similar murder of two doctors about a year ago. They were decapitated and skinned. Their penises were cut off, and those, along with the heads and skin were placed neatly under their open throats. The scene was clean as a whistle except for the trail of blood to the drain. I reviewed the preliminary reports this morning, and it has the same basics. Just one big difference: there is a bullet hole between his eyes."

Eddie was listening intently. "Did you find the murderer last year?"

Gus shook his head slowly. "Lexi was out of town at the time, and we were snowed under, so she was recalled and assigned to it. The latest murder she was working on was resolved, as I understand, and was connected to the doctor murders last year, but I don't think there was proof of their murderer. There were questions about Mr. Castanzo, the mutilated body up the hill, but I don't know the details. I usually work in the computer area, and now that Lexi is missing, they've called me in to help. Believe me, this is not my idea of research."

***

Lexi had passed the Castanzo gate on her way down the mountain that morning, and she knew she had done everything possible to balance her life by trying to kill Castanzo. She knew she and her twin had different outlooks on crime and punishment, but this one just felt right. Gram had been her life until she discovered Cyanna at a Pow Wow. After becoming so close, her own thinking had been influenced by her sister's insight on protecting your own. When she read the paper, she knew Cy had worked her own balancing act again. Lexi's feelings of gratitude to her twin and the deep loss she felt overwhelmed her. She knew she must find a place for her and her little wolf Wyya, so she pointed her Jeep north toward the beginning of a new life.

***

Back in his sports car, Eddie dialed Chicago. At the message tone he said, "Hey. I've just been by the murder scene. I haven't been able to see any of the reports, but I met one of the CSI agents, and he let me know that this murder is just like the ones last year on your nephews. So, when Tony called last week letting you know there was a female problem close to his home he was going to fix, it looks like she fixed him. I'm wondering if she killed your nephews, too. Anyway, I'm on it."

II

Cyanna awakened with the sunrise. Her eyes were almost sealed by eye crud. She gently rubbed them with her forefinger knuckles, when her mouth dryness and body aches screamed for attention. Slowly rising, she stretched, and said, "Well, Daddy, I'd better get some help here. I am in pain all over. I miss you. Almost forgot, Lex calls me Scooter, just like you always did. I thought you'd like that."

The young woman walked through the gate to the surrounding wrought-iron fence and locked it. With helmet strapped, she straddled the Harley and fired it up. She blew a kiss, and said, "I love you, Daddy." She put the bike in gear and slowly pulled away from the plot.

A local courtesy area gave her a place to freshen herself, and a nearby restaurant offered coffee and breakfast. She gassed up the bike and headed out of town.

***

Lexi cuddled little Wyya while the pup nuzzled the inner part of her master's neck. With hands cupped under the puppy's furry butt, she rocked her back and forth. She sang, "You Are My Sunshine." Gram used to sing it to her when she was a child to comfort her or help her go to sleep.

The young woman was still replaying in her mind the day Gram was killed. The pain enveloped her again, and tears slid down her cheeks and bubbled on top of Wyya's fur. She remembered the break in by Castanzo's thugs, and how the wolves fought and died beside her and Scooter. She saw a side of her twin she had never thought possible. The way she used that knife was amazing, almost frightening. Then, after she had admitted she was the one to butcher those doctors last year, Lexi surprised herself that she actually didn't blame her. She understood the feelings of betrayal and fury when the doctors destroyed their father and drove Scooter to murder because the same feelings took over her own rationale and drove her to try to murder Castanzo. She thought, *I wonder which-Native American or British-heritage makes us so rigid in thinking that we must balance our lives by destroying those who hurt our loved ones.*

Scooter had left that morning after they had camped out not far from the mob boss's home, and Lexi had awakened from her nap with Missie Wyya. Lexi still couldn't believe that *there was only one wolf left after having so many at the fort.* Thoughts about what must be done were carefully organized. She had tethered the pup, pulled on the nitrile gloves, and taken her grandfather's prize .45 to load with the round lead and powder.

The young woman had arrived at the Tudor mansion in the early evening on her bike with every intention of killing Castanzo, but what she found was that Scooter had already arrived before her.

"What are you doing here?" Scooter asked a little surprised."

Startled, "Well, I'm happy to see you, too. I'm going to kill that son-of-a-bitch," she responded as she reached for the .45 in her fanny pack.

"Lex, look, let me take care of this." Scooter parked the Softtail and walked over to her. With no warning, she took the gun right out of her hand.

"Don't you think I can kill someone?"

"Lex, it was hard for me to tell you that I murdered those doctors last year, and I don't regret it. They needed killin'. What I didn't tell you is that killin' is easy after you first do it, and I don't want that for you."

Castanzo couldn't be roused on the intercom. "Where do you suppose the asshole is?"

"I don't know, but don't you worry, I'll find him. You'd better get back to Missie Wyya. I've got this."

Reluctantly, Lexi had started to leave on her bike, but dismounted and approached Scooter and grasped her shoulders. Tears involuntarily escaped from the outer corners of her eyes, and she asked, "Where will you go?"

"I'll probably head for the only home I knew before I met you and Gram: Oklahoma."

III

Arriving at the fort, Gus set his new work kit down, opened it, and pulled on nitrile gloves. Heavy gauze covers for his shoes were more for the shoes than protecting evidence with all the soot on the ground. A walk around the perimeter showed him he would need a ladder and more sealing containers for specimen because most of the burned fort had ended up in the basement.

The officer remembered visiting the fortress when Lexi had had her birthday celebrations in recent years; he had missed the last one. He never quite understood the whole Pow Wow situation, but Lexi always seemed more settled after. He thought of the ingenuity behind the building of the fort: the care of the grandparents planning for the wolves by having the ladder access from the back of the house and into each room. He loved the wolves, too, and noticing so many bones and pieces of fur piled up near the center of the basement floor, and with none of the wolves evident, his eyelids welled with tears. He thought, *how could this have happened? Did this have anything to do with the cases Lexi was working on?*

The crunching cinders slowed him down. He carefully made his way to what was once the kitchen entry. There he realized he would not find any really defining information. The devastation was almost complete.

Gus went back to his kit, checked his digital camera, and popped in a new memory card. He panned the area from each side of the fort and took close up shots of the driveway, surrounding yards, and the interior of the building that was possible from the exterior perimeter. He labeled the memory card and placed it in a hard plastic holder. He pulled out his sketch book and drew a rough draft of the wreckage.

The bones in the basement were not easily accessible, so he decided to go back to the lab and pick up a ladder and maybe someone to help him gather them. Since this was new to him, he hadn't thought to bring all the equipment he needed. He really hoped he wouldn't find any human bones even though he expected to.

Once in the lab, the officer found the ladder he needed, but everyone else was working on the Castanzo murder scene; the grounds were extensive. He wondered if there was the possibility that some information he needed from the case Lexi was working on might show it was connected to the fire.

Gus walked slowly to Lexi's office, paused, and took a deep breath before he opened the door. He could smell her fragrance hanging in the air. The room was very clean and organized; even the desk mat was orderly. On top of it was a copy of her report dated the week before. He pulled the chair back and sat down slowly. He sighed, with elbows on the desk put his face in his hands, and began to weep. Tears ran down into his hands and dropped onto the desk mat. A short time later he regained his composure, blew his nose on his handkerchief, and addressed the report in front of him.

The lab results and the written report spiked his interest. The spreadsheets that he had prepared for Lexi and the dental spreadsheets from the college were of particular interest. He had already explained them to Lexi, but there was a sticky note on the top that indicated the college spreadsheets were obtained by Scooter. Gus knew that was what Lexi called her twin. *So, that's how she got them—through her sister who worked at the college.*

Gus turned on Lexi's computer and didn't take too long to figure out her password, given his expertise and her focus in life. He found her private notations that Castanzo was somehow behind the murder of Dr. Rebecca Byrd, the dental director at the college. *So, he may have had something to do with the fire if he knew Lexi was on to him.* Then he found the report of Lexi's discussion with Castanzo at the office that confirmed his suspicions.

Gus made notes on a small pad, turned off the computer, and went to his office to see if there was more information on Scooter. He found nothing, because the girls must have different last names. He made a mental note to go by the college to find out her real name. He loaded up the ladder and plenty of specimen bags and headed back to the fort.

Once there he carefully placed the ladder in the basement and made his way down to the pile of bones with his kit in tow. He pulled on nitrile gloves and began to bag each bone separately. He worked into the evening, loaded up his findings along with the ladder, and headed for the lab. By the time he arrived, it was late and he decided to begin on the evidence the next morning.

On awakening, Gus realized he could make a swing by the college and check on Scooter's name. He arrived at the college and walked past the downstairs lab that he didn't realize was the murder scene a year ago. No one appeared to be around, but he heard people talking and followed the sounds.

"Any of you know Scooter?

The small group of maintenance people looked at one another and questioned, "Does he work here?"

Gus smiled and said, "She works in dental hygiene."

"Oh, you mean Cy. Her name is not Scooter; it's Cyanna Ansley. I'll show you her station, but I don't think she's here today."

Gus followed the young man to the work area that was designated by a name plate "Cyanna Ansley." He made a note and planned to look her up on the computer as soon as he got to the lab.

On arrival, the officer logged in and pulled up an information site he used often. He was surprised to find her address prior to Lexi's was not far from the city. He thought *it shouldn't be too hard to find in a small town* and as soon as he had a spare moment he planned to drive out and track it down.

The lab work was tedious, but he soon sorted out the animal bones from the human bones. By the end of the afternoon, he was relieved to know that there was only one human skeleton and he knew it couldn't be Lexi. The femur was too short. *It must belong to Gram.*

After a shower and a new set of scrubs, the photographs were next. He printed all photos in 8" X 10" format, and transported them to the conference table to take a look. Nothing jumped out at him, and he had in the back of his mind the possibility of finding out more about Scooter aka Cyanna Ansley. It was late, and he didn't think anyone would be available for conversation with a stranger, so he decided to wait until the morning.

IV

The road out of town into the mountains was on the opposite end of the city from the fort and turned out to be a relaxing drive except for the haunting questions about the disappearance of Lexi and Scooter. Gus thought, *maybe Scooter knows someone out here that the girls could stay with, that is, if they* are *together.*

As Gus entered the small town, he felt a peace that seemed to emanate from the open valley surroundings. The speed limit slowed the traffic, and the passengers in the cars waved at one another. *You wouldn't see that in the city,* he mused.

At the first service station, he asked directions to the street address and if anyone had heard of Cyanna Ansley. He was told that the turn-over of residents was not that much, but he should check with the neighbors along the street. It wasn't hard to find the comfortable looking ranch style home. He drove under the arch in front of the property, parked in the driveway, and approached the heavy rustic door.

The door opened slowly and a fragile, elderly lady with a walker joined him on the entry. Smiling she said, "I've been watching you. You must be new to the area or lost."

"I've been trying to find any information about Cyanna Ansley. This is the last address we have for her. I'm sorry, I should have introduced myself; my name is

Gus Ferguson. I'm a crime scene investigator with the city." His badge seemed to mesmerize her.

A few moments later, she said, "We bought this place from a very sad young lady. Her name was Cy. Beautiful. Was on that motorcycle every time I saw her. Reminded me of myself when I was young, her fearless abandon. She gave us a great deal on this place. My husband reminded her of her father who had just passed away." She slowly shook her head from side to side, and carefully sat down on her walker seat.

"Can you tell me anything else about her?"

"The two of them built this place, and then he got real sick and passed. I don't know where her mother was, but you could tell they took good care of each other. My husband and I love it out here, and her generosity and fairness with the sale helped us to be able to enjoy the last few years we have away from that crazy city."

Gus thanked her for her time and returned to his car. Out of curiosity, he drove back to the cemetery he had noticed on his way to the ranch. Slowly he drove by the gravesites noting the names. As he turned the corner into the Native American area, he saw a Jeep like Lexi's across the grassy area on the eastern most part of the site. A young woman was kneeling as she placed a bouquet of red roses in front of the stone. As Gus came closer he could read the name on the back of the stone: ANSLEY. He noticed she had her head down and was moving her lips as

15

though she was talking to someone. The officer didn't want to intrude, so he parked at the end of the road.

Gus walked quietly up the road and as he approached the Jeep, he heard a low growl coming from a very small wolf tethered in the back of the Jeep. Aware of the warning, Lexi turned and came face to face with the man who had always loved her. Lexi's red eyes, wet face, and broken demeanor were welcomed into his open arms; he forgot himself and circled her spirit with his.

Lexi had just lost everything in the world that meant anything to her except Missie Wyya, and Gus knew he had a second chance at happiness. It didn't matter what had happened at the fort, he was thankful, relieved, and thrilled she was still alive.

After a few moments of holding one another, Lexi leaned backward, but Gus wouldn't let her go. She began rambling, "This is my father I never knew. When I found Scooter at the Pow Wow, you know, that day I was recalled from my vacation, I never thought I would ever want to know anything about him because I always thought he had abandoned me. Gram would never talk about him until Scooter came to stay with us. Then she told me the story about my dad. Evidently he stole Scooter from my mother just after she gave birth to us. Scooter loved him so much and we've talked about him a lot; I feel I know him and I can't help being like him. At least, I'm like Scooter and she is just like him, she says."

Lexi took a deep breath and looked up into his eyes where she saw what she had never let herself see before.

His blushing face had always kept her from recognizing the sentiment that had caused it. Her reflection peered back at her and she felt the love from him she had mistaken for years. The difference in their heights made a small problem, but not for long. He gently picked her up by the waist and with her hands resting on his shoulders, their lips touched ever so slightly.

Small volts of pulsating electricity were exchanged and felt throughout their bodies as their parted lips connected. They both forgot to breathe.

When they came up for air and released their grip on one another, Gus said, "Then you know where Scooter is?"

Guardedly Lexi, responded, "I haven't seen her since the weekend. I don't know where she is."

The investigator insisted, "What in the world happened after SWAT was there?"

Lexi extricated herself and walked a few feet away before she turned to face him. Through her mind she quickly replayed the last few days; she knew she wouldn't betray Scooter, but she somehow wanted Gus to understand. *So, how can I explain?*

"What just happened here? Isn't that a little more important than what transpired a couple of days ago?"

"I am so sorry, Lexi. Part of me died when I thought you were in that charcoal mess that used to be the fort. I can't even believe my luck in finding you again. I apologize for showing my feelings, but I have waited too long to tell you I love you."

V

The next morning Lexi opened her eyes slowly. *What have I done?* The last thing she remembered thinking was, *it won't fit.* *At least, Gus didn't ask any more questions about Scooter.* She got up quietly without disturbing him, dressed, picked up Wyya, and escaped.

She knew she should have waited to explain, *but how could I tell him what I've done?* To have started the fire in the fort to release the spirits of Gram and the wolves the way she knew Gram wanted was against all she had learned as CSI. She knew he would want more information about Scooter and she couldn't go there.

Lexi had been ready to leave town when Gus found her, so she started the Jeep and headed north out of town. She didn't notice the black sports car turn in behind her as she left the motel.

***

Scooter had been riding for a couple of days toward Oklahoma. She was trying to decide what would be best to do. She yearned for the comfort from Gram, Lexi, and the wolves. Tears shed on a motorcycle only cause mucus leakage and burning eyes, but she couldn't help herself. She had to stop. She pulled over and was overcome by emotion.

The young woman was determined to have a fort and a new pack of wolves. There were two tasks ahead. Money was not an issue because of the sale of the ranch and her father's life insurance funds placed in money making entities, so *no more tears: start with a real estate person and an architect, then on to a reservation to find someone with wolves.*

***

Gus awakened with a smile on his face. He rolled over, and stretched. His hand started patting the covers and he sat up with a start. Lexi was gone; so was the pup. He couldn't believe he'd found her only to lose her again. Stumbling with one leg in his pants, he quickly opened the door to see if her Jeep was gone. He was exasperated, *how did I not feel she was gone!*

The drive back to town was quiet as he searched his soul about what had happened. Spending the rest of his life with Lexi would have been the dream he wanted to live. Last night had been part of that dream that now seemed lost.

***

Scooter rode slowly through town. It reminded her of the place she and her dad had built their home except that there were big trees everywhere. The weather was muggy, so she figured the dampness from growing the trees had something to do with it. As she crossed what looked like the main part of town judging from the traffic, a campus emerged. At first, she wasn't sure if it was academic, federal, or state. A little further and she knew this was the place for her new job. She didn't need the money, but working would take her mind off the past and she could establish herself within a community again.

Parking for visitors wasn't hard to find and she didn't need much room anyway. She locked her helmet on to the bike and noticed the different buildings. One in the center of the complex looked like an open forum, so she started there. Just inside she found a dispatching office and asked the way to human resources.

The building was fairly new and in immaculate condition. On the way, she passed bulletin boards advertising housing, classes, and future Native American Pow Wows.

The human resources office had a warm atmosphere. The young lady who greeted her answered her queries about availability of jobs. The openings wouldn't be until the fall, but now was the time to apply and interview.

Scooter found the local library with computers open and plugged in her flash drive to pull up her resume to attach to the internet job applications for positions available at the new facility. She posted where she was qualified.

While she was typing, the murder came back to her. She was curious; the first murders had bothered her for a few days even to the point of having nightmares, but this one she hadn't even thought about, even on the long ride, since she left the castle when she bid him farewell with her usual *you're legal now* thought.

Scooter remembered she had parked her bike up the road behind a full grown fir tree, so it couldn't be seen from the highway. She had scaled the fence and checked out the grounds as quickly as possible. All was quiet in the castle, with no movement except for the horses in the field. She finally determined Castanzo was off site.

Back to her bike, Scooter fired it up and travelled the road to the favorite look out. As she rounded the corner, there he was: binoculars in hand pointed in the direction of the fort. The embers were still smoldering. She thought, *he must wonder why his body guards didn't return.*

A safe distance away, the young woman contemplated her options and decided to wait for him to return to his lair. She drove back to her earlier hiding place, parked the bike, and carried her supplies to set up surveillance near the gate. After she had left Lexi napping with Wyya, she had made a trip into town to pick up the necessities for the legalization. She had her grandfather's loaded .45 and his knives. The knives were not quite what she was used to, but they were long enough and he had left them razor sharp.

Castanzo must have had a meeting somewhere or went for lunch because it was couple of hours before he drove into the entry. That gave her time to change into her ceremonial attire. The slow closure of the gate insured

Scooter's easy access. She was careful to stay behind the trees and was waiting for him when he stepped out of the limo on the circle driveway. He had had to drive himself because he had sent both body guards and his butler/chef and horse caretaker, who were accomplished Marshall Arts enthusiasts, to visit the girls.

Scooter said, "Hi."

Castanzo couldn't hide his shock at seeing the beautiful Native American in her long leather beaded gown. He knew she looked familiar, but the regalia led him off the path and he didn't immediately connect the young woman to the ones he had ordered killed. He was aroused and had trouble thinking logically.

The mobster's response was, "Hello, there, yourself. How the Hell did you get in here?" He looked around and remembered he was alone.

"I followed you in," was her answer. She captivated his eyes with hers until she could see the glimmer of recognition creeping into his consciousness. He first saw the .45 when she let it slowly slide from behind her perfect butt.

"I want you to walk very carefully into the entry," she said calmly as she pointed the muzzle of the gun directly at the center of his head.

"What do you think you're doing?" he demanded.

"I'm going to make you very legal. Now, no more talking." She cooed.

Scooter remembered she motioned him toward the tall Tudor doors of the entrance. She sensed the gears in his mind were churning. He walked slowly; almost to the doors, he suddenly turned and challenged her. The bullet caught him by surprise and made a nice round hole between his beautiful eyebrows. The momentum forced his back against one side of the giant doors. He gasped and tried to speak as his arms flailed and his legs gave way; the body slid down the doors so he was in a sitting position.

Scooter said, *"Too bad you won't be awake for the best part of your legalization."*

VI

Lexi was driving out of town when she noticed a flashy black sports car following her. She realized she was going to need ice so a stop by the market seemed in order. The sports car stopped, too.

Missie Wyya secured, the young woman went into the store and bought the ice. As she added the ice to the chest, a handsome young man walked over to her and asked if she needed any help. She thought, *he's as tall as Gus.* She told him she had it under control and he went on his way.

Lexi drove off; a few minutes later she observed the same sports car behind her. It followed her for miles. The desert area she had to travel was barren with long distances between towns or rest stops. She was a little spooked because every time she checked the rear view mirror, there was that same car. She finally had to stop at a rest stop. She let Missie Wyya do her business and retied her in her seat.

The sports car had stopped also. Lexi wished there were people around, but she had to use the restroom. As she quickly finished and washed her hands, the tall young man from the sports car walked around the corner blocking the only exit.

A cape of fear engulfed the young woman. She looked up into the jet black eyes that showed no emotion.

"What's your hurry, Beautiful?"

"You are in my way." Lexi said with sudden dry acidic mouth.

Lexi realized too late she should have brought her gun or waited for another more populated area, but he had been following her for hours and she had to go.

Eddie reached for her and she backed up. "You leave me alone!" she screamed.

***

Scooter had found a quaint old bed and breakfast for the first night; she slept fitfully. She needed a place to pull the bike in so she wouldn't worry about someone messing with it. But it almost seemed like more; she wondered *if Lexi and Missie Wyya are safe.* She had a strange feeling she couldn't describe. Then *maybe it's just because last week I was with my family and now I'm not.*

The next morning, a trip to the post office to check the bulletin board for places to rent and see if her face was on the Federal Most Wanted poster seemed in order. She wasn't on the list, *not that I really care, just curious.* She left the building and found a real estate office, parked the bike, and walked inside.

Seated at the desk was a very large Native American; Scooter knew she had to be Cherokee from the tan skin, high cheek bones, and coal black eyes and hair. She was dressed in jeans and a colorful tunic decorated with heavy silver jewelry.

"Hi, there," she greeted as she raised her palm toward her visitor.

"Hi, Yourself. I have two requests," Scooter returned. "I need a furnished place to rent where I can pull my bike in out of the weather, and I need acreage to build a fort."

No show of emotion came from the proprietor. "I can help you with both. My name is Moon." She rose and walked to the vertical file in the corner behind her desk and retrieved two folders. She laid them on the desk and sat down carefully. Scooter took a seat and placed her helmet on the floor.

Moon offered the young woman several photos of property and addresses for rent. After a few minutes, sites were chosen that seemed to be possibilities. They agreed that Scooter would follow her on her bike to take a look at the properties.

Not far from the center of town, there was a one story duplex in an area where the buildings appeared to be older and the yards were well kept. Scooter parked her bike and walked up to the door. A thin, older lady with a white bun and many years on her face smiled as she opened the door. The pain of loss shot through the young biker. She tried to concentrate and not remember Gram; a lifetime had traveled through her soul in the last few days.

"I'd like to take a look at your rental." Scooter offered.

"Just let me get the key," the little lady said. She left the doorway for a few moments and soon returned. Walking very slowly with use of a cane, she made her way to the entrance of the duplex that was separated from her half of the building by the driveway into her garage.

Scooter ventured to say, "Would the noise from my bike leaving and returning bother you?"

Verna Magnus replied that she had been a bit wild in her younger years and never regretted one minute of it, especially now that she was having trouble just walking.

The duplex was clean with one bedroom, one bath, and access from the garage door into the kitchen with linoleum flooring where she could park her bike, if necessary. The garage would be fine, but if her paranoia mounted, she could pull it inside. There was only one outside door, the front door. Scooter liked that, too.

Ms. Magnus was delighted to fill her empty duplex with a young biker. She saw the adventure in the young one, and that made her feel younger. Scooter agreed to the rental terms and signed the papers that morning.

The real estate broker had waited patiently and led the way to available acreage. Just like her grandfather, Scooter knew the place when she saw the land butt against the shear face of an unusual mountain that stopped abruptly at the top with no access available and could serve as one side of the property. In one day, Moon had connected a renter and an owner to the perfect properties. *It was a good day.*

Scooter set in motion all the paperwork and asked about architects. With a couple of calls, she had an appointment to discuss her new fortress. Excitement was not really one of her allowed privileges, but the inner hope for the same comfort she had felt with Gram and Lexi made her anxious. And that nagging feeling from last night just wouldn't go away. She wondered *if I dare call Lex on her cell.*

VII

Lexi awakened in a daze. She was chilled deep into her bones; she had been lying on the concrete inside the rest stop ladies' room for hours. It was dark with only the glow from the outside lamps. Wyya was whimpering. Movement seemed impossible, but she finally made it to her feet. Thoughts invaded her, *Oh, nooo!*

The realization of the violation almost knocked her down again. She cradled her abdomen with her hands and began to weep and moan. *How could I have let this happen? Always on my guard, and I even knew he was following me.*

Missie Wyya could hear her crying. The whimpering turned into howling, and Lexi knew she needed to take care of her. She slowly staggered to the Jeep and painfully climbed into the driver's seat; she was greeted with lots of gentle kisses from the pup that made her realize the extreme throbbing in her face. Lexi felt reassured by Wyya, but she knew she needed some care. A look in the rearview mirror sent terror through her; *I didn't see his fist coming.*

The little town had no emergency room, so Lexi had to drive back to the big city.

***

Eddie felt he had taken care of business with Lexi. The information he had found in the file on her desk assured him that she was the one Tony had described when he called his old man. He had had no trouble finding her office. *If she was the one who killed my cousins it makes perfect sense because Tony was killed the same way; if she wasn't the one, it doesn't matter. She was just a broad and good for only one thing, anyway.* He wasn't sure she was dead, *but after what I did to her she should be dead.* He turned back to the city to see if he could get any more information from Gus.

The young Italian was congratulating himself on the way he followed Gus from the mountain to the office and then to this town on a hunch that he might find something. Sure enough, he found the one they were both looking for. That's all he really needed, even though, he did have to wait all night to get to her.

***

Gus had made his way back to the office; he was at the lowest point in his life. *How can I go on?*

***

Lexi arrived at the hospital emergency room in a daze. A visit to another rest room had been an effort and was pure agony. She knew the report of the rape would bring attention and medical testing.

It wasn't enough to go through the ordeal of degradation, but now to have the most personal part of her life invaded again. She knew what might happen; the whole department would be alerted because she had been missing since the fire at the fort. That night with Gus was there *with the memories of euphoria* she had never experienced before. Then the insane nightmare with the same act was not logical. She wasn't thinking clearly, but she needed attention to her jaw. She thought, *it's broken.*

Lexi needed to talk to Scooter and yearned to have her near. They had an unspoken understanding that they weren't to use their cell phones, but given the circumstances she was tempted.

The emergency room was swamped. There had been a roll-over accident involving a bus and a tractor trailer rig, so to get any attention was pure luck. A young intern didn't ask many questions and ordered an x-ray of her jaw. The results were no fracture, so he added several stitches. When he finished and no one was paying attention, she left.

***

Scooter settled into her new digs where she always brought the Harley inside the kitchen; she moved the table and chairs up against the wall, so the bike had the place of importance in the room. Ms. Magnus and Scooter seemed to be very pleased with the new set up. The first few days the older lady brought cookies, then cake, then on another day, dinner for the two to share. The practice became the norm. Verna was lonely and just being around the young biker made her feel better.

Scooter received the call to interview at the state center. The job was that of an assistant to a group of ladies who set policy for accreditation for college curriculum in the state. The workload would be about the same as she had had for the dental hygiene program when she lived with Gram and Lexi.

During the meeting, her first impressions of the committee she would be working for reminded her of particular professors she worked for at the dental hygiene program. She remembered there were some who were genuine and always there to help students, but it only took a couple to poison the department. They were all "Type A" personalities, and after she had worked there for a few months *she knew that A stood for Anal.* She was always amazed how such intelligent people could be so mean and nasty to one another.

One day, two professors would team together in favor of one professor and sing her praises based on her work performance or her interaction with students; it seemed like the very next day, the same two would be trying to get her fired for doing the exact same thing. Then in the middle, those two would break off and find a new compatriot to conspire against a different faculty member. Or one of the original conspirators would go to the professor in question and tell her she was the object of the current attack and rat out her former partner!

The main problem with this scenario was that supervision was advised of the low level of focus the professors had on the students when they were spinning their webs, and they did nothing about it, so the students were the ones to suffer. Then, there was always the way they treated the support group. It didn't matter if they had the same education or more; if they weren't on the same echelon of teaching, they looked down their noses at them and treated them with distain and disrespect.

Scooter had had enough of the ugliness that people do to one another, so she wasn't really sure if she should take another job with all females, but maybe these would be different. And she wanted to be part of a community and try to find the kind of connection she had at Gram's and when her father was alive. The fort was being planned, and she really didn't have much to fill her time, so she accepted the position.

VIII

Scooter couldn't shake the feeling that something was wrong. It was strong and always there in the back of her mind. Working at the new job and daily seeing Ms. Magnus kept her busy, but not really focused. Her relationship with her landlady was pleasing and helpful while she was trying to heal from the loss of family, but it was going to take time.

Then Scooter began to think, *why can't Lex and I be together? It's been almost nine months and I'm not on the Federal Most Wanted list. So what if I am caught for what the liberals think is murder? We could be happy until then.*

The building of the fort was almost to completion, mainly because the money was available and she had stressed to the builder the importance of immediate occupancy. The young woman thought that maybe when she was settled, that nagging feeling would go away. It was almost like she herself was in danger.

Scooter had worked for months trying to please the staff, but she found herself always turning the other cheek. Given her particular skill with a knife, she wondered *why do I put up with them?* She had been right: it was very like working at the hygiene school. There were turnovers of leadership which always made work difficult for her and she commented on it one day while talking to one of the members. She said, "I don't think anyone understands how these turnovers impact me and my work."

The associate looked directly at her and proclaimed that "no one cares what you think." There was no waver in her voice; she wasn't angry. She just stated a fact.

Scooter mused, *that's kinda what I thought,* but what she said was "I'm really glad you cleared that up for me, and while we are on the subject, I was wrong to have thought so highly of you and the staff." She turned the power off to the computer in the middle of a document, stood up from her computer chair, took her fanny pack from her desk drawer, and left the office.

That afternoon, the supervisor was looking for her. She never returned. She had left the hygiene school and not returned; this was no different.

Scooter did some soul searching on her way out the door. She wondered why she had been trying to work anyway, *maybe for the benefits, the health insurance and to be connected with the community. Not enough reason to be disrespected as a human being. The first time was the fault of the dental hygiene school faculty; this time it's mine for agreeing to work under the same conditions. There won't be another. Time to move on.*

Before she fired up the bike in the parking lot, she pulled out her cell, clicked on Lexi's number, and waited. *Just to make sure, I'm going to put to rest this nagging feeling along with the aggravation of this job. Maybe I can find peace.*

Lexi was lying on her bed and heard what she thought was her cell phone. Surprised to hear it ring, she had to investigate its location, and she had a difficult time getting off the bed. The baby had taken its toll on her body; she couldn't breathe, lie down, sit, eat, sleep, walk or do anything comfortably because of the size of her abdomen. Moving quickly was out of the question. She had been isolated for months living on the savings she and Gram had in their joint accounts. She had wanted to call Scooter since they left the mountain, but she thought they might be caught or her connection with her twin might get Scooter caught.

The cell phone was in a bureau drawer under her underwear. As Lexi picked it up, she could see that it was her sister's number.

Cautiously, she answered, "Hello."

Scooter's emotional tide made her voice falter, so that Lexi repeated herself. "Hello. Is anyone there?"

A deep breath and Scooter began. "How are you? I know we probably shouldn't be talking, but I've had this nagging feeling since the day after I left the mountain."

Lexi began to weep quietly. As the tears slid down her cheeks, she tried to speak, but the words wouldn't form. Blubber was all that was audible.

"Lex, what is it?" Scooter implored.

The mother-to-be finally recovered. "Scooter, something has happened. I need you."

"Where are you, Lex?" That nagging feeling was now full blown terror, not the rush she felt in a fight, but the kind one is helpless to remedy. Before her sister could answer, Scooter was breathing quickly and she had a strange taste in her mouth.

"I'm not far from where we left one another. After I saw you at Castanzo's that day, I went back and picked up Missie Wyya. We drove to the little town where our father is buried, and I spent a couple of days there. Oh, Scooter, I can't tell you what happened over the phone. Where are you?"

"I'm in a little town in Oklahoma."

"I can't travel that far right now."

"Why? Are you sick?"

"Well, not really."

"Lex, you are talking in circles. What's wrong?"

The twin didn't hesitate. "Give me your address." Lexi gave the information and Scooter knew exactly where she was; she had lived in that little town.

Scooter said, "I'm on my way." Lexi collapsed on her bed sobbing.

IX

Gus had left the area where he had found Lexi with no direction in mind. He knew he had to complete his case work, but he was determined not to involve her in the end result. He was an honest man and was having ethical issues about the final report he had to submit to his superiors.

The report that was submitted was filled with exact data citing his scientific findings. There was really no connection to Lexi other than she was alive and he found no reason to add that to the report. He had second thoughts about it over the next few months, but could not justify his written findings with her existence.

Gus lived very frugally and slipped into a deep depression, barely making himself go to work. He took off days sporadically, but he had so many hours of sick leave, he could have been gone for months legally. Those off days were the days he couldn't make himself get out of bed.

***

Eddie, on the other hand, had elevated himself in the organization by killing the woman who had killed his cousins; at least, that's what he told everyone. The old man, his father, ran the Chicago faction with an iron hand. When the sons of his sisters were murdered the year before and in such a grisly manner, he hadn't been as focused as he was when Tony, his main connection to several money making areas, was murdered in the same way. That was one reason he sent his son to find out what he could; the other reason was his sisters were badgering him. (He had to remind himself that family was important even if it was a female.) It was very helpful to have Eddie in the police department for more reasons than being able to visit other police stations across the country.

Eddie's new assignment was to contact Gus periodically to see if any progress had been made in finding the body of the woman he killed. He was not surprised to realize that Gus was in love with the girl he called Lexi, especially after witnessing the way he acted that morning on the mountain by the fort. Every time he talked to him, he seemed sadder. He kept calling just to follow through with his old man's orders; he knew that rest stop was far out of the way and not visited very often, but *still someone should have found her by now.*

Eddie went on with his life and married the woman his father picked out for him, the daughter of a powerful politician. The mob boss crossed more lines of decency with his plan to have a grandchild connecting him to government legalities. After several months, there was clear disappointment that a child was not on the way.

***

Scooter rode home, packed what she needed, including her knives and her grandfather's .45. She explained to Verna that the job was going nowhere and she had to make a trip. They also talked a few minutes about the fort being close to completion and the fact that she wouldn't need the duplex any more. Verna was sad about her trip and her moving. She managed a little smile as the biker fired up the machine and rode off.

Riding at night can be a blast, but Scooter tried to focus. She knew something terrible had happened because she had been feeling it for months. It seemed weird to her that she and Lexi were connected by some kind of knowing power. *I should have called her sooner*!

The trip was complicated because of the weather. It was still winter and not the best time to travel on a bike. Instead of the two day trip, it was closer to four. She did stop one night because of the blowing snow. Exhausted, she found a motel where she could bring the bike inside.

Deep in a dream, panic seized her; sweaty and wide awake, she sat straight up in bed. Lexi was being attacked. The twins were in a very dark and cold cave, and Lexi was screaming from far away. Scooter was running blind as fast as she could, crashing into jagged rocks at every turn.

Then there was blood, and she couldn't tell if it was hers or Lexi's. Scooter had only been asleep for a short while, but the wind had stopped blowing and the traffic was moving on the highway. She knew she couldn't sleep more because *I have to get to Lexi.*

***

The day was beautiful with full sun and cold temperatures for the quiet little town where she had spent so much time. There was no wind yet, but the spring weather would bring more than is comfortable. Scooter rode directly to the street Lexi had mentioned.

There was a small cabin to the side of a large brick home with Lexi's Jeep parked by the door. It had its own chain link fence and Scooter could see a full size grey wolf behind it. She pulled up to the front of the cabin and parked her bike. As she was removing her helmet, Lexi opened the door, and Missie Wyya gave a welcoming yelp from the yard.

Scooter couldn't believe her eyes. Lexi had gained weight, and she looked like she had a basketball under her shirt. *Oh My God!*

"What in the world happened?" Scooter asked as she leaned forward and hugged her sister. Lexi returned her care and they held one another for a long moment. Lexi began to weep.

"Lex, you've got to tell me what's going on!"

They went inside where Missie Wyya had let herself in through the back door. She bounded to meet Scooter who opened her arms and was met full force with the weight of the adult wolf. They hit the floor together and rolled and played like they had at Gram's fort. Scooter felt at home and secure.

After a few minutes, the twin extricated herself from the young wolf and turned to Lexi, who had made fresh coffee. As they added sugar and cream, Lexi tried to begin her story.

"Scooter, I read the newspaper the day after Castanzo was murdered. All the report said was that he was mutilated. I have the paper if you want to read it." Scooter agreed to read it later, but she wanted to know how this baby came about.

Lexi began, but all she could really get out was, "I was raped!"

Scooter, immediately flushed, and furious that she hadn't been there for her sister said, "Who is the son-of-a-bitch?"

Lexi sipped her coffee to steady herself, and began again. She told Scooter about the visit to

45

their father's grave and the meeting with Gus. She told her that the sex was natural because even though there had never been anything between them before, once they knew they loved one another, the love making was spontaneous and beautiful.

"So, Gus is the father? But that's not rape. Then where the Hell is he?" Scooter was baffled.

"Well, I'm not sure, and I couldn't contact him anyway because of maybe giving him information about you." Lexi edged.

"What do you mean, you're not sure?"

"I was followed when I left town the day after I saw Gus. I knew I was being followed, but I had been driving all day and I had to pee. So, I stopped at a road side rest center and he caught me in the restroom.

X

Scooter could feel anger begin to override her objectivity. An unforgiveable offense against her only living relative had possibly put Lexi's health in danger. She looked swollen and uncomfortable, and *who knows what that being inside her would do.*

"What does this guy look like?"

Lexi, tried to move through the horror of the memory and how she had tried to scrub herself raw every time she thought about the violation. "He was as tall as Gus, but he had black hair and eyes. I remember those eyes, so black you couldn't read them. You know that saying that the eyes are the windows to the soul. I think his heart is as black as his eyes. I thought he was handsome the first time I saw him."

"When did you first see him?"

"After I left Gus, I stopped at a convenience store just outside of town and bought some ice. He came up to me and wanted to know if I needed any help. I told him no, but I noticed he followed me the rest of the day. I know I shouldn't have stopped at that remote area, but I was about to burst."

"Did you notice anything about his car?"

"It was a black sports car. You know I'm not into cars, so it could have been any kind, just black."

Scooter said, "That's no help." When she saw the sad look on Lexi's face, she said, "Don't you worry. I'll find this piece of shit if it takes me the rest of my life. I'll make him sorry he invaded my family." Lexi felt sorry for him already because she knew her twin.

That evening they talked well into the night relaying to one another what they had been doing the last few months. They talked about their unspoken agreement not to call on the cell phone, but now they were together they realized there was no reason why they shouldn't have been together, and now more than ever they needed one another.

Lexi told Scooter the details of the rape: how panic seized her brain so completely she couldn't think clearly, and that it was a good thing he knocked her out, because she would have fought him to her death. The humiliation of knowing that she had been violated in the worst possible way haunted her daily, along with the possibility of the baby being the result of the crime; but she never lost hope that maybe the baby belonged to Gus. Abortion was not a consideration. She always had believed that babies have the right to life regardless of the circumstances of their conception.

Scooter could see the scar on her jaw from the stitches, and she had to tell herself that there was a better time for her to address the anger that kept rising within her. Lexi told her about Missie Wyya being in the Jeep and that she could probably recognize the puke's smell.

The mother-to-be shared that after she left the hospital for the assault, she realized she would have to be close to the city where she knew where everything was and her health insurance was honored until it ran out, so she decided to stay in the little town. She had run into a few people who thought they knew her, but of course, it was Scooter they knew. She always told them that everyone has a double somewhere. The job she had at the bookstore, where she was paid cash, helped keep her mind and hands busy, and it supplemented her savings to provide for Missie Wyya and the baby.

Scooter told her she need not stay there because the fort was near completion and they could move in any day. Missie Wyya would be the beginning of their new pack. She told her about the job she had had and the bitches she worked for. The computer system at the facility was run very like the one they uncovered for the dental director and the doctors that Lexi had investigated. One of the programs tracked the money for the program, and she had found how they misappropriated money and paid for offsite training and vacations using funds earmarked for state use. As a young woman, Scooter had trusted that people in higher positions were honest; now having worked for two different state institutions, she was convinced anyone who could use the system for their own benefit, did.

Scooter and Lexi felt that they were at home, so it wasn't the place. They had one another and Missie Wyya. The girls moved the mattress from the bedroom to the living room floor and talked well into the night. The next morning Missie Wyya awakened them the way she always had: by cleaning their ears with her tongue. Scooter had missed the wolves and totally enjoyed the process and the giggles.

The girls agreed that it was time to be together, and nothing would ever come between them again. The baby's birth was very close, Lexi terminated her work at the book store, and Scooter called the builder to see how close the fort was to completion. She let herself be excited for a moment; her new home was finished and she was bringing her family to live there.

Lexi had rented the little house furnished, so there wasn't much to the moving. The bulk of necessities were for the baby and the Jeep had to have room for Missie Wyya, who now always sat in the front passenger seat. Lexi had sold her Sportster when she first settled in the small town, so the area reserved to carry it on the back of the Jeep could hold any portion of necessary items she wanted to take with her.

The twins discussed thoroughly the possibility of the baby being born on the way, but they really hoped they could make it to Oklahoma to be his birthplace. Lexi didn't have a sonogram, but she always had the feeling that the baby was a boy. She didn't know if Gus was the father or if he was the result of the rape, but she held on to the hope that this baby was a Ferguson. She often wondered *if Gus ever thinks about me.*

***

The telephone rang in the lab where Gus was working on a new case. "Ferguson here," he answered.

"Hey, Gus. How the Hell are you?"

"Hi, Eddie. I'm the same."

"No word about the Castanzo killer? How about that co-worker you lost?"

Gus had begun to wonder why Eddie kept calling, so much he recognized his voice, and he always asked about Lexi. If he didn't know he was a cop, he might think there was an underlying motive.

He replied, "It seems after studying Lexi's files and notes that the dental director was killed by a dentist in a mental facility. At least, he had the tongue that was removed, and he had access because he could come and go as he pleased, and his little girl who had been admitted to the facility had been treated inexcusably by the woman. The dental director was connected to Castanzo years ago, but none of that has anything to do with the way the mob lord was killed. He was murdered the same way as the doctors a couple of years ago except for the bullet hole in his head, and I still don't have any leads on that. The crime scenes were too clean. I think Castanzo was afraid Lexi had found a connection to the director about him, and that's why he sent those men to destroy her. We connected those four stiffs at the fort with him. And no news about Lexi.

You will be the first to know because you are the only one who continues to ask about her." *Maybe Eddie really does care.*

XI

Lexi's condition was uncomfortable, but she had never felt more alive and happy since she was a child. The ride would be chilly, so she covered her legs with a blanket in excess of her hooded jacket and gloves. She was anxious to be safe in the new fortress, and Missie Wyya was eager with the expectancy of a trip in the Jeep riding shotgun. Scooter would follow Lexi on the Harley in a pre-planned itinerary.

The first day was calm and cold. They stopped at each rest stop for Lexi to get the circulation going in her legs and pee with Scooter standing right beside her. She wasn't embarrassed; she had to get past the fear somehow, but for now she needed the moral support. This little boy was draining every bit of nutrition out of her body. They made good time without much traffic and found a motel after about eight hours. There was just enough room for the Harley in the entry.

Lexi was fatigued. She didn't want to eat and went right to sleep. She slept soundly until daylight when Missie Wyya awakened both of the girls with her same appealing way. Scooter took the wolf for a walk to do her business, and when she returned Lexi was trying to get out of bed. She had to laugh.

"I'm not feeling very well right now," Lexi explained.

"Is is time for the baby?" Scooter asked.

"My due date is tomorrow, but I may make it a little longer."

"I hope you can hold on until we get to the Oklahoma border."

"I don't know if I have any control over it. I've never had a baby, and what I understand is that when he decides to be born, he will be born."

The twins loaded up and began the journey again. The weather held and they traveled for another long eight hours. The border was just in reach, but Lexi was in distress. She slowly exited the Jeep cradling her heavy abdomen. She collapsed just as she made it to the bed.

"Why didn't you tell me sooner that you were in trouble?"

"I thought I could make it all the way to the border. It's not that much farther." Lexi rolled onto her side and moaned.

"I'm going to get us some dinner. You didn't eat last night and that's not good. You need to stay strong."

"Scooter, I can't eat. Just let me sleep."

The young biker walked and fed Missie Wyya; then she walked over to the nearby diner and asked for takeout. When she returned, she found Lexi in the bathroom. She said, "My water broke."

Anyone observing could have seen the puzzlement on Scooter's face. "What do you mean your water broke? Are you okay?"

"My contractions have started. The baby is coming." Lexi came out of the bathroom determined to continue the journey, so the boy could be born in Oklahoma.

"We have to rest. Besides, there's a hospital here."

"My son is not going to be born just anyplace. We have to go." Scooter knew her sister was very like herself and once she made up her mind, nothing would change it.

"Lex, I have to find a place for my bike and I'll drive you. I'll be right back." Scooter ran all the way to the office. She had noticed the grey-haired manager had tattoos, and she thought he might understand what she was going to suggest. *Folks who ride Harleys are good people; they just have a bad reputation sometimes because of the few who give bikers a bad name.*

"Hi. I just rented #14. I would like to rent it for the next few days. I am going to leave my bike inside, just so you know. My sister is about to deliver her baby and she wants him born in Oklahoma, so I'm going to drive her. Hopefully, I can make it in time."

"You don't have to rent the room. I have a bike trailer I won't be using again. You can have it. Is that Jeep set up for towing?"

"It is. I insist on paying you for it."

"Let's hook it up and get you going. I'm just happy someone can use it. I'll go check the tires and you bring the Jeep around back."

Scooter hurried back to the room, got the keys to the Jeep, and drove it around to the garage of the motel. The manager, walking with a limp, helped her hook up the trailer and gave directions for the closest way to the border. He hoped *she doesn't have to deliver the baby on the way.*

Scooter pulled in front of the room, loaded the bike and secured it onto the trailer. She called to Lexi and Missie Wyya. The wolf was in the Jeep in a bound and Lexi was ready, but she was moving very slowly. Her sister helped her into the back seat and took pillows from the room for her comfort. She checked the room, left three $100 bills, jumped in the Jeep, and took off. A stop at the corner station for gas and drinks brought them to departure within half an hour of Lexi's demand.

The contractions were getting closer together when they saw the signs that welcomed them to Oklahoma. Lexi relaxed and the pains seemed to hasten. Breathing became panting and the pain made her shriek. Scooter thought, *that son of a bitch is going to pay when I catch him.*

Scooter kept asking her sister if she needed help. Finally, Lexi said, "I think the baby is coming. You'd better stop and help me." Scooter pulled the tandem as far off the road as she dared.

The young woman had lain down so she could have her feet flat on the seat and her legs could part easily. Scooter thought she could see the baby's head in the opening and went quickly to the bike saddle bag and retrieved a short roll of plastic. She covered the area under Lexi's bottom and tethered Missie Wyya who had begun to whine. She pushed the passenger seat forward and out of the way and pulled out the blankets and medical supplies Lexi had packed for the trip.

The grimace and beads of perspiration on Lexi's face verified the pains were excruciating and the birth was imminent. Scooter had pulled on nitrile gloves and had her hands ready for the baby. Within her, she was worried if she could help her sister, but she assured Lexi that all would be fine. A glance in the direction of Wyya almost let her miss the child as he shot out of his special home. Struggling for control of the slippery body, she caught him and covered him carefully with a blanket leaving only the cord extended.

"Sounds like a boy to me," the surprised sister said as the little boy screamed. "Lex, have you got your work cut out for you. That noise will drive me crazy." Once the baby was laid on Lexi's abdomen, she pulled him to her face and began to weep. He was suddenly quiet. The storm that had threatened was at bay, and there was total silence.

Scooter, all business, noticed the quiet and stopped to realize there was an aura of mistiness: she had just witnessed a miracle and almost missed one of the most awe inspiring moments of her life. Her demeanor softened, and the tone of her voice changed. Watching Lexi with her new son hit her abruptly with a new responsibility.

"Do you want to cut the cord?" Scooter finally asked as she started to hand the knife to the new mother, but decided she would do this herself. She completed the cleanup of mess, mother, and baby, and added blankets to keep them warm. In the distance she could see lightning, and she swore she heard a chanting.

XII

Scooter turned her head to one side to better hear the chanting when she noticed Missie Wyya was standing with her head turned to one side. She seemed puzzled by the sounds that traveled across the open land between them and the mountain. There was a flash of lighting near the mountain that showed the outline of what Scooter thought was a teepee. Both girl and canine watched patiently for the next burst of light.

There was no doubt; a teepee appeared in the distance every time the lighting flashed, and the sounds emanating from it were a mantra. Scooter started to speak to Lexi, but could see she and her little man were sleeping.

A decision had to be made. Scooter could drive to the next town and come back to investigate this unusual citing, or she could go now. She wondered *if my sister is okay.* She wasn't running a fever, and all seemed fine. *What if she takes a turn for the worse? Then what?*

Scooter added the bagged birthing debris to the trailer with elastic cords. She untied Missie Wyya who immediately began to run toward the sounds and the teepee. She first called to her; she stopped for a second but continued. It was not like her to disobey. She switched on a flashlight to see the wolf running toward the mountain. There was no road, so the young woman wondered if there were canyons or crevasses between the road and the teepee.

She knew she would be taking a chance if she drove the Jeep with her precious cargo, but her gut feeling was that she must follow the canine.

Although it was dark, Scooter quickly released the cords holding the bike to the trailer and backed it off. It didn't take long for her to locate Wyya. The wolf had run directly in line from the Jeep to the wigwam. There were many obstacles of shrubs, cacti, and deep ditches, but they were more easily missed on the bike than they would have been in the Jeep. It was a short ride.

On arrival at what had appeared to be a teepee, she could not believe her eyes. She didn't dismount, but shut off the engine. Warm light from the intermittent lighting seemed to glow around an older, grey-haired Native American squaw dressed in an aged skirt and tunic. The subdued colors showed both had been worn for many years. The elder lady was only as tall as Missie Wyya and was standing in front of her with their noses almost touching. She turned her head toward the young biker and said emphatically, "askai usdi asgayv!!.

Scooter's mind raced. She couldn't remember her Cherokee.

"Askai usdi asgayv!!" The little person repeated.

Scooter knew she was tired, worried that she had just left Lexi unprotected, anxious to get Wyya back, thankful she had not run into any complications with the quick trip getting there, but now that this woman who was so much like Gram was demanding something. *What the Hell is going on?*

"Who are you?" Scooter demanded as she glanced back toward the Jeep and could see no traffic or anything because of the dark. Just then, the surrounding lighting gave her a glimpse of the Jeep. She felt better that she saw it and returned her attention to the little old lady.

"Askai usdi asgayv!!"

The feeling of jeopardy was suffocating. She glanced in the direction of the Jeep. There were headlights shining on it. Some vehicle had stopped there, and she could see silhouettes of at least two men approaching the Jeep.

Scooter whistled to Wyya and fired up the bike. Fear she had never felt before took her by the throat; *think, where is the gun—in front of Lexi on the floor where she had laid it—where are the knives—one in each boot, one hooked to the pocket, the others in the saddle bags.* The bike flew across the distance to the Jeep.

Frank and Harry Johnson, ages 41 and 40 respectively, stopped at the Jeep because they thought they had found a fortune. Their mom had kicked them out of the house earlier because she knew they had taken the grocery money and spent it on beer. They didn't have enough gas to make it back home or to the nearest town, so they had stopped behind the Jeep and discussed first stealing the gas; then they decided if no one was there and it didn't appear anyone was there, they'd just steal the vehicle, especially if it had more gas than their old truck.

The light from the truck disturbed Lexi, and she roused. Then she heard the men arguing about the trailer. They were talking about how to remove the trailer; neither knew how to disconnect it. They both heard the motorcycle and looked up about the time Scooter arrived.

Engaging the kickstand with her left foot and dismounting slowly, the young biker said, "Can I help you with something?"

Frank, the elder brother, hooked one thumb in his dirty overalls and began walking over to the biker. He felt very confident because his brother Harry had a crowbar and he had his hand on an old pistol in his pocket. *Besides this is just one woman.*

Scooter took a few steps to the side of the Jeep, so she could glance in to check on Lexi and the baby. The headlight reflected off the barrel of Grandfather's .45 in the new mother's hand. *Free to deal with these assholes.*

"Nope. We saw this here Jeep and thought we'd take it off yourn hands."

The young warrior noticed the outline of a weapon in the pants pocket of the speaker. "It's not for sale." She stated flatly.

The men began to laugh; they laughed so hard they threw back their heads unaware of Scooter's silent reach for knives from the side of each boot. The delivery was swift as she quickened her step and leaped into the air beside the puke to pull the blade across Frank's neck. He grabbed his neck in shock with his free hand and his knees buckled as he landed face first into the dirt with his other hand still in his pocket. Wyya appeared from out of the darkness to attack Harry full force in the chest and knock him to the ground. As he raised the iron to hit her, the young woman plunged the knife straight into his heart. Without hesitation, she checked for pulse and wiped the blood off her weapons on the fallen idiots.

"Lex, you okay?"

"Where have you been!?" The baby started to scream.

Scooter quickly loaded the bike and strapped it down with enough light from the headlights of the old truck. Then she turned them off careful to hit the button with the butt of her knife; the door had been left open. She jumped into the Jeep with Wyya right after her on the other side.

"Lex, I really can't explain anything just yet. We've got to get on the road."

Lexi sat up carefully, adjusted herself with the pillows, and offered her breast to the little one. It seemed very natural and he was quiet again. They traveled in peace until they reached the next town.

XIII

The storm caught them with the first town another couple of hours, but there was a rest stop within a few miles. Scooter helped her sister to the rest room while Lexi carried the baby. Wyya stayed close.

"We'd better go to the emergency room just to make sure you did a good job and to register the birth." Lexi explained. She wasn't worried, but wanted confirmation.

"Are you thinking you are not well?" Scooter asked.

"Actually, I feel better than I have for a long while. I just want to make sure everything is in order."

When they were back in the Jeep and pillows were adjusted so Lexi could feed the baby, they had time to talk.

"Scooter, thank you, for taking care of us. I know this is all new to you, but you did a pretty good job except for the diaper was backwards. That's fine, because you will be an expert before he doesn't need them anymore."

"You were awesome. I can't even imagine the pain you were in, something that big coming from a place so small." After a long silence, she said, "Were you aware of any of that scenario back where we stopped?"

"I know we were in trouble. I heard those voices and froze. I couldn't figure out where you were. Then I realized the gun was there on the floor board. I gripped the .45 because I thought I was going to have to shoot them. And did I mention I was scared out of my britches, which I didn't even have on?"

"Do you know what happened after I came back on the bike?" She didn't let her answer. "Lex, I am so sorry I left you, but you were sleeping, and the most bizarre thing happened. Wyya and I both heard a chanting, like a mantra, from what I thought was a wigwam toward the mountains. I could see the outline of it when the lighting would flash. I knew I shouldn't leave you, but it was almost like an invitation to the unknown, like a puzzle or a riddle. I was strangely drawn. Anyway, I took the bike because I didn't want to jostle you two around. It's a good thing, too, because the terrain was a test for that big bike."

"You were lucky you didn't break your neck riding in the dark with no knowledge of the area. So, what's the mystery?"

"Missie Wyya took off running toward the noise, which is not like any of our wolves. I found her with a little old squaw in front of a lighted area; from the road, the shape was like a teepee. She spoke in Cherokee, but I couldn't make out the words except askai. And sure enough, there was good reason for fear. I turned around and came right back. We had to leave the area in a hurry because I executed those two pukes."

"Did you have to kill them?"

"I thought they were going to murder us to take the Jeep. I didn't really have time to bargain with them," she stated with a stern voice.

They travelled without talking for a while when Scooter said, "When we have time I want to go back to see that little person. I could have sworn it was Gram before I got a good look at her. I want to know how she knew about him to sing the mantra and why she was so in tune with us. She said her name was Adanvdo." She paused lost in her own thoughts. "So who does this little boy look like?"

Lexi was looking at the baby when a passing car would light the cab. "The long black hair could be from our side, but I think he looks like Gus. And how did he get that black spot on his forehead? "

"What black spot?"

"It looks like a smudge from a black cooking pot or charcoal."

Scooter said, "I'll take a look when we stop. So, what are we going to call the little guy? "

"Should we name him after our father or our grandfather or maybe his own father? Lexi pondered.

"Should it be Cyrus or Alex or Gus? Are you sure he's not that asshole's issue?"

"We aren't going to discuss that asshole from now on, Cyanna. And he doesn't even look like him. He is a mini Gus."

"Oh, Boy. I know you are serious when you call me by my name. Very well, then. I'll just say one more thing and I won't mention him again. I **will** find him, he **will** pay for what he has done to you, and I **will not** tell you about it, but I won't have to, you'll know."

"Cy, can't you just let it go? We have our little guy now, and I will need your input the rest of his life. I don't want anything to happen to you."

Scooter flipped her cell open and left a message for the builder to call her the next morning to see when she could move into the fort. Then she said, "I think we should call him *Ahwi Usdi*. That way we would incorporate Ahwi our mother's surname just as our grandfather used his mother's surname. We could spell his first name a little differently so he wouldn't have so much trouble in school. How about A, W, I, A, H, W, I."

"Little Deer. You don't think he'll be teased in school? Let me think about it."

They arrived in town and asked at the first service station about the hospital. The directions were easy, and they were soon in the hospital emergency room. The doctor on call checked Lexi and was impressed that she had delivered with no professional help, but he realized the mother was Native American and he saw many of them after delivery. The baby was cleaned, weighed, and measured. The paperwork was completed and all were wished well by staff as they left.

The name on the birth certificate was **Gus Ferguson Ahwi.** As Cyanna looked over the draft that had to go to the state office, she approved. The original would be sent to the post office box near the fort. She vowed *to call him Awi Usdi.*

XIV

They found a nice motel and settled in for a good rest. Cy pulled the bike inside and Wyya found her own place between the beds. The new aunt encouraged Lexi to shower carefully, while she introduced herself to Awi Usdi.

Cuddling the bundle, Little Deer was sleeping; his breathing sounded like a kitten purring. Cy was smitten. Never had she held a baby, and this one was her family. Canines had always snuggled with her throughout her life, but this was different. The transition of love from her father's love to Gram and Lexi seemed necessary given the circumstances of her dad's passing and new found family. But, this little boy was defenseless and totally dependent. And he was so soft and he smelled so good. His long black hair was straight and stood at attention on top. She thought *it is curious that a Native American baby can have blue eyes, but that's probably from Gus or maybe from Dad.*

Lexi came from the shower to find Scooter sitting in one of the chairs with the baby in her arms; both were sound asleep. She nudged her sister and pointed out that she could drop him. Scooter helped her sister into bed with the baby. She lay down on top of the other bed without undressing or removing her boots. Exhaustion took over both girls, and they slept until Little Deer was hungry again.

A couple of hours of sound sleep helped both girls. The storm had continued with a vengeance. Wind, rain, sleet, and snow kept them within the confines of the room sleet, and snow kept them within the confines of the room for the next couple of days. Scooter left the room for supplies and trips necessary for Wyya. The builder called to say the house was ready for final inspection and an appointment was needed. A time was agreed on within the next week.

The twins had time to rest and get to know the new baby. The time not sleeping was spent talking about the times they had with Gram, the way she loved them, and how they missed her. Scooter remembered the little squaw and that brought up the discussion about the smudge on Awi's forehead.

Scooter said, "You know, I've been thinking. As soon as we can travel, I'm going to take a trip out to where I saw the wigwam. That black mark on his head reminded me that maybe the old lady was one of the little people that help Cherokee folks. She had really long grey hair, and remember, I told you I thought it was Gram before I realized how short she was. Maybe they knew about the trouble coming, and that was their way of warning us."

Lexi turned her head to one side as if she were trying to figure what was wrong with Scooter, and said, "What little people?"

"Don't you remember from Cherokee lessons that the little people help children in trouble, and Awi sure fit that description. They knew ahead of time those pukes were coming."

71

Lexi decided to humor her sister and let her believe whatever she wanted to believe and dropped the subject.

Missie Wyya paid attention to the little one and appeared to be surprised by the noise that came from him. She seemed to like the way he tasted because she was always licking his cheeks and gently poking his chest with her nose.

Lexi recovered well and when the weather permitted, Scooter made a trip out to the birth site on the bike. The police had been there and gone, but there were still dark spots in the dirt where the pukes had bled out. She crossed the area to where the strange triangular light should have been and could find nothing, not even evidence of a fire.

The bike trip proved nothing, so they traveled deep into Cherokee country to check out the new fortress. Lexi was resting with Awi in the back seat of the Jeep as they arrived in front of the fortress. She stirred when they stopped. As she rose to a sitting position and saw her new home, her eyes opened wide and a thrill of excitement caught her off guard. She said, "I can't believe it. It looks exactly like Gram's!"

Scooter stepped out of the Jeep to meet the builder who exited his white, king cab truck in front of the building. They shook hands and proceeded toward the structure. Lexi reminded her sister she needed a little help by calling to her. She came back and helped her out of the

Jeep. As they approached the man, she introduced him to Lexi as Rex.

Rex was tall and broad shouldered, blond and blue-eyed, and very handsome for his older years. He wasn't too old to notice the striking beauties that were about to inhabit one of his finer building endeavors.

Together the twins walked into the entry. They turned to look at one another; there were memories clouding their perception of the new structure. Scooter had made changes that were not immediately evident. As they continued from room to room, Rex pointed out the levels of stronger composition between the walls that were at least two feet thick, the steel encased bullet proof windows equipped with electronically monitored steel shutters, and the steel reinforced doors with an opening big enough to level a rifle through. Scooter had gotten the idea from an old fort she had visited near the border. One could close the opening or balance a rifle barrel through it to shoot outside.

Lexi stayed on the main floor while her sister and Rex checked the basement. The overall effect was the same as Gram's fort except the ladders became narrow steps; Scooter had noticed how hard it was for the older wolves to navigate those in Gram's basement. They still opened by overhead doors into each of the upstairs rooms. Scooter told Lexi to remind her to see an extra she had added to the basement when she was ready to go downstairs.

Scooter inquired about finalizing the paperwork and the date they could move in. Within the week they had the utilities turned on and began camping in their new home.

XV

The next few weeks were filled with shopping for furnishings, and the girls were amused by their nesting attributes. Scooter had gone to great lengths to prepare for an onslaught of terror that they had lived through once, and inside the fort they felt comfortable and safe. Missie Wyya, having been cooped up in the Jeep or a motel room for several days, romped in her new compound. In the night, she howled her loneliness.

The twins talked incessantly about Gram, the wolves, the break in, the future. Little Awi appeared to be the smartest child ever born. The girls were certain he was the only child to have ever pushed himself up on his forearms during the first week of his existence. By the time the furnishings began to arrive, one would never know which young woman had given birth to the baby. Lexi had regained her figure, and both girls acted like Awi's mother.

The fort became a home. Even though they worked together, Lexi spent more of her time making their home comfortable and more like the one they had burned in respect for their grandmother. Scooter spent her time making sure no one would be able to attack them as before. She had had the builder place hidden cupboards big enough to conceal weapons near the protection holes in the doors for her knives, ammunition, and guns. She sharpened her new knives and cleaned her new firearms and kept them loaded, except for the .45. An advanced burglary system was installed that still allowed the entrance through the trap doors of a being less than 70 pounds. None of the wolves would surpass that weight, and if they did, she would address the issue.

There was always time to play with Awi. When the girls were busy, they laid the infant on the floor on a pallet, and Missie Wyya would take care of him. She would lie very close to the pallet and if he stirred, she would begin to howl quietly. The girls would drop what they were doing and run to him. Together the four of them took a break and the family unit became closer to one another each day.

Lexi loved her little boy and after a few months, his blue eyes stayed blue, and his dark hair turned blonde. He was Gus, just a lot shorter. Lexi missed her baby's father and yearned to tell him about Awi. When the twins talked about it, Scooter cautioned her.

"You know he would want to see him, but he is still CSI, and has probably figured out by now that we burned the fort. Would he understand why? What is he, Irish? He would not understand Native American culture rituals."

"I know, but a father should know his own flesh and blood." Lexi would counter. "You remember that case I was working on with the director?"

"Hello. I was helping you. Do you remember?" Scooter looked at her as if she had lost a few years.

"Sorry. I just meant that the father—you know—Superman, he was so protective of his little girl, even when he wasn't all there mentally he thought if he cut out the tongue of the person who kept verbally abusing her, the pain would stop. And he didn't kill the director, she had a heart attack; however, if someone cut out my tongue, I might have a heart attack, too. I want Gus to know his son. Our dad knew you and probably didn't know about me. He insisted on knowing his own."

"You do whatever you think is right, but I'm on record that you shouldn't let him know about Awi. You're just asking for problems."

***

Mornings were happy with the family unit. Awi and Wyya dominated the twins' lives. Days were busy and the nights were restful.

Awi was almost a year old and the girls had plans to celebrate his life with a Pow Wow at the fort. It would be fashioned after those that Lexi had after her grandparents had finished their fort.

One night a couple of months before the celebration, Lexi and Scooter were awakened by Awi's screams. They were both by his bed in a heartbeat. The little body was writhing with muscular movement for him to bring the curdled milk from his stomach. He was scared from his convulsive vomiting. They took turns trying to make sure he was upright so the stomach overflow would not be breathed in. They tried to calm him down. After hours of walking with him partially draped over their shoulders, he finally went to sleep.

Scooter and Lexi both began by trying to figure out if he had had something different to eat. They checked his little body for bites or a clue to what had made him ill. The following day they were tired from no sleep, but the day went by fine and Awi was playing and "talking" to them in his own special way.

That night they gave him his bottle and he went right to sleep. Scooter checked the perimeter with Missie Wyya and the twins started to have a night cap when Awi awakened from a sound sleep trying to vomit again. The next day they went to his pediatrician. Something they told him made him order several tests at the main hospital in Oklahoma City.

The next weeks were mingled with Awi vomiting every night, no sleep, worry, and frustration because the testing found nothing wrong with Awi. He began to lose weight and interest in his surroundings. Looking at him showed a frail, listless baby. There was no "talking" or cooing anymore. Missie Wyya would lie as close to him as possible and whimper periodically. She knew something was wrong.

"We can't just watch him die!" Scooter was angry. "Damn doctors don't know what they're doing. They just want to charge for expensive tests and tell you they didn't find anything, so the patient must be fine. He is NOT FINE! We have to go to another clinic."

"The best one is where we just came from. Do we dare go back?" Lexi was on the verge of tears.

"What choice do we have? If they are going to catch me, oh well. I'd murder those sons-of-bitches again if I had the chance!!" Scooter slammed out of the house.

Both twins knew she was not angry with Lexi; it was the whole situation. Their life was so complete with Awi, and to have the family together meant more than life to them. She knew she had been stupid to stay away from Lexi in fear of being tracked down by the police because that's when Lexi was raped.

As she paced, she reflected with a sense of accomplishment. The compound had really shaped up. The nine foot chain link around the perimeter made the acreage become a unit. The security light in the center could illuminate the entire area. The entrance into the basement was well camouflaged. As she walked around the yard with Missie Wyya at her heals, she knew she had done a good job making a home for her loved ones. She knew she would gladly sacrifice any material assets she had gained to have Awi well again. *We have to go back.*

XVI

Lexi made the arrangements to see the specialist; the travel plans were set up. They wouldn't leave Missie Wyya, so they were going to drive through. Scooter loaded up the Jeep, closed up the fort, and set the alarm.

Missie Wyya was excited about a road trip. The twins knew they would be fine because they had made this trip with more against them than what they had now. Awi seemed to take to riding in the Jeep. The vibration from the tires put him to sleep. If he had a bottle before he slept, he would wake up vomiting. They took turns driving and taking care of Awi.

The first day they passed the place where Awi was born and Scooter had killed the idiots. A look across the terrain between the road and the mountain showed them nothing out of the ordinary.

That night they stopped at the motel where they had gotten the trailer for the bike the day Awi was born. The manager was delighted to see the baby; he had wondered if they made it through to Oklahoma for his birth. The old biker told Scooter that she shouldn't have left such a big tip in the room; he said his maid couldn't stop bragging about it.

The girls rested a few hours, but the worry about the baby was always foremost in their minds. One would sleep when Awi was sleeping; the other drove. The decision to drive the rest of the way without stopping at a motel served them both well. The short naps seemed to help them more than the miserable nights they had been having.

Several hours later, the big city loomed before them. So many memories invaded their minds; they were both quiet for a long time. Finally, discussion about location of the quarters where they would stay brought them back to the present. The building was across the street from the renowned hospital. It was the same hospital where their father had passed away.

Scooter and Lexi signed in at the desk and unloaded the Jeep. They showered and organized their room. Laundry from Awi's spit-up needed to be done immediately or it would sour more. They had asked for a room with easy access to the small garden area where they could walk Wyya, so a trip there was in order.

The appointment with the specialist was not for another day, so the girls decided to make a trip up by the fort where they had spent an important part of their lives.

The next morning, they were surprised to find the ruins of the fortress still with police perimeter tape. The goldenrod strips were damaged and flying in the wind from different areas around the site. The girls looked at one another and tears welled in their eyes. Gram and Ugia and Wyya. The fire and Castanzo's goons. A moment was all they needed. Scooter thought, *Too bad he didn't feel more of the pain he gave.*

The drive to the top of the mountain was cold, but they had no problem with the roads; the Jeep was equipped. The snow had been plowed to high banks along the side of the road. The tree tendrils were heavy with new fallen snow that sparkled in the morning light. The air was brisk and soothing, peaceful. Wyya ran and played bouncing in the snow like a pup. Then they started down the mountain and passed the home of the late Tony Castanzo.

Back at their temporary home, Lexi asked, "Do you want to talk about the Castanzo thing?"

"No. It's history."

***

Gus was in deep concentration trying to track who had deleted information from his data base. He knew he could find it; it would just take time because there is always a link to deletions. The telephone rang. "Ferguson, here."

"Hey, Gus. How are you?"

"Is that you, Eddie?"

"It is. My wife and I are in town and would like to have dinner with you. Got any room in that busy schedule of yours?" Eddie smirked.

"You know me. Pick a night." Gus was trying to pull himself away from his project and pay attention. He had wondered about Eddie and his occasional calls. He knew some people think differently than he did, so *maybe Eddie is just fishing for information, but what?*

They agreed on a time and place that evening. Gus dressed in a suit and even a tie. He didn't know what to expect.

***

The same night maneuvers with Awi kept Scooter and Lexi busy until the next morning when they made sure Missie Wyya was comfortable before they left for the doctor's appointment. Scooter and Lexi carrying Awi walked across the street to the hospital.

The doctor greeted the girls; he did a retake when he realized the twins were identical. A handsome man of fifty, he knew this was one time he was pleased he worked out regularly. However, he had Awi's charts and had them sit down in his office to go over the details that might not be in the written notes.

Lexi explained how the vomiting attacks had begun after she weaned him from the breast at around ten months, and the steps the other doctors had suggested along with the testing that had all showed them nothing. The doctor said he wanted to be honest and could really not give them anymore information until he made more tests. He took Awi into another room to do a physical exam with the girls following.

Little Deer had lost weight and appeared to be just a little bag of bones. His eyes were dulled and he didn't make any move to object to the doctor invading his comfort zone.

Watching him, Lexi began to weep. Scooter put her arm around her shoulder, and tears escaped from her own eyes. They knew they had to be strong, and they had been through so much. But this little guy that meant so much to them both needed their help, and they felt helpless.

The doctor pretended not to notice the tears. He said, "There are a couple of tests that haven't been done. Also, do you have medical information from the father?"

The twins were stunned. They looked at one another and couldn't believe they hadn't thought about that. *Maybe what he has is linked to his DNA!*

Appointments were set up beginning that afternoon. Ordinarily, it takes weeks for testing to be scheduled, but the doctor was concerned that the little guy was going down hill fast.

It was lunch time, so Scooter asked where the cafeteria was and they started walking toward it.

XVII

Gus had been pleasantly surprised with Eddie's wife. She was about as tall as Lexi, but not nearly as attractive. He thought, *she's really pale.* She was blond and different from Eddie in almost every way. She didn't share personal information while her husband blew his own horn. It seemed very important that he let Gus know he had the best of everything and could buy whatever he wanted.

They ordered dinner and were eating when Jennifer asked to be excused. She was gone a long time. The men finished their dinner and were contemplating dessert, when the waitress brought them a note. It was from the ladies' room where Jennifer was in distress. Eddie left to check on her while Gus paid the bill.

Eddie called Gus on his cell to say he was taking his wife to the university hospital. Gus told him he would meet him there.

Jennifer had a miscarriage, and although she wasn't admitted to the hospital, she was in the emergency room well into the next day. Gus had stayed to support Eddie and they were just going up to the cafeteria for lunch when they turned the corner and came face to face with Scooter, Lexi, and Awi.

All stopped dead. The silence was deafening. Scooter didn't understand the sudden stop and she didn't know the men. As she touched the baby in Lexi's arms, almost like a defense mechanism, she slowly raised her eyes to peer at her sister's face. Lexi was looking at Eddie, and the horror she experienced that night was written there. As Scooter followed her eyes to Eddie's disbelieving eyes, she knew instantly that he was the puke she had to deal with.

Gus couldn't find words. The feelings he had the last time he found Lexi were all mixed together. He and Eddie had been up all night discussing the fact that Eddie and his wife could have more children and how important is was to Eddie's father to be a grandfather; he wasn't sure if he was actually seeing her. As he glanced at Eddie, he saw something he had not seen before; he appeared to be unsure of himself. It was somewhere between surprise, disappointment, and anger.

Eddie was surprised to see Lexi alive, he was disappointed she wasn't dead, and he was angry with himself because he hadn't cut her throat to make sure she would not live.

Awi began to squirm. Gus's heart was pounding so hard, he thought it might burst. It had been about a year and a half. *Could this be my baby?*

Scooter broke the silence as she slowly started to reach for the knife in her boot. "Is this the son-of-a-bitch, Lex?"

Lexi could see what was coming and tried to intervene. As calmly as she could muster, she said "Gus, this is my sister Cyanna."

Gus immediately noticed the ugly scar on Lexi's face. The other girl looked more like his love. *What is going on here?* He ignored Lexi and spoke to Scooter. He said, "Where have you been? I haven't had a minute's peace since that night."

"Look Dude. I'm not Lexi. She is. Lex, is that the son-of-a-bitch?" she demanded as she glared at Eddie.

Awi began to pitch a fit. "Scooter, we've got to go."

"Not before you answer me."

Lexi screeched, "Yes, that's the son-of-a-bitch!"

Scooter lunged across the minimal distance between them, grabbed Eddie's shirt collar at the neck with her left hand, and slammed him up against the wall with her other hand and body weight. He was surprised at the strength coming from a woman. It was a turn on instantly and his involuntary libido poked her in the stomach.

Scooter snarled viciously with her face barely an inch from his, "You'd better enjoy your pecker because it's not long for this world." She backed away not taking her eyes from his. She and Lexi continued backing away fast with Gus protesting and Eddie trying to calm his body part.

Eddie thought to himself, *too bad I picked the wrong twin; that one would have given me more of a fight.* To Gus, as if he didn't know, he said, "Who the Hell was that?"

"You tell me, she didn't seem very happy to see you. What did she say?"

"I didn't quite catch it." He lied. "You knew them, right?"

"That was Lexi and Cyanna. I knew they were twins, but I didn't realize how much they looked alike. And there's a baby. I never told you, but Lexi and I had a night together several months ago. I know you kept asking about her, but I really didn't have any news. This is the first time I've seen her since. I wonder if that baby is mine."

"You'd better get your department to track where she lives so you can find out." Eddie's ulterior motives were already at work. He thought, *lose one baby, get another. Hey, that could be my baby. That might solve my problem with the old man.*

XVIII

Lexi and Cyanna took Awi and left the hospital. Lunch was forgotten. They didn't talk until they were back in the room. Missie Wyya was delighted to see them, and Cy took her for her short walk to the garden.

When the two of them returned, Cy said, "We have to have the testing done, you have to talk to Gus about his family, and we can't stay here. Any ideas?" She was pacing.

"Maybe Gus can help us." Lexi was hopeful and scared, but excited about talking to her lover.

There was little time before the first test, so there wouldn't be a break for them. Awi was changed and fed before they headed back for the hospital.

The testing took all afternoon; Scooter was worried to leave them alone with the predator in the hospital. Between the later tests, Lexi called Gus and asked him to meet her in the lobby. She left her sister in charge of Awi for a few minutes with the father of her child.

***

As Lexi approached Gus in the large windowed waiting room, her heartbeat began racing. All the months being apart had given her ample time to think through the events of that night and the next day when Awi was conceived. She had thought about the time carrying Awi and the worry that he would be the rapist's child. The decision to keep him regardless of whose issue was worrisome right up to the moment he was born. Then there was no question. Love between a child and the mother poured into her heart and consumed her. She now understood her father for taking Cyanna. She thought, *a father has the right to know his child.*

Gus was elated that Lexi called him. He had been so depressed over the last months. Excitement kept him agitated until he saw her.

Both had been trying to think of the right words, but once they saw each other whatever they had been thinking left them. They stared at one another with only a few inches between them. They both started to speak at the same time, then stopped. Their arms circled one another and kept them close for several moments. Hands together, the couple walked to the corner of the waiting room.

Lexi started, "I've wanted to talk to you ever since that night, but I didn't really want to get into the whole burning fort explanation. I was afraid you'd ask the questions I didn't want to answer."

"Don't worry about that. I cleared up the report without bringing your name into it. I want to know where that baby came from. Is it yours?"

She couldn't help herself. "He's ours."

Gus felt like a huge bubble of water had washed over him. Pure joy and relief imbedded itself within his being. The smile seemed to cover his whole body. Unable to contain himself he pulled Lexi to him and kissed her full on the lips. Moments went by.

"Tell me about him. What's his name, when is his birthday, when can I see him?" He had so many questions; she couldn't answer them fast enough.

"His name is Gus Ferguson AHWI, and we call him AWI, shortened for my maternal sir name that means deer. Scooter delivered him along side of a highway in Oklahoma. Afterward we went to the nearest hospital and both he and I were checked out."

Still beaming Gus said, "Why are you here at the hospital?" Lexi explained about Awi's illness and the testing necessary. She asked him if there was anyone in his family that had any of the symptoms.

Gus was amazed. He said, "I had the same type of problems after I was born. I was sickly until I was about twelve. My mother had tried several different foods and found certain ones I could tolerate; I slowly regained my strength, but I never gained much weight. I had, and still have, an immune deficiency disorder. I know you haven't had time to inspect my body without clothes, but I still have patches of dryness related to skin disease that is a part of it."

"But Awi doesn't have the dry skin."

"He will. I started out the same way—not being able to eat, vomiting up my bottle feedings. I questioned my mother when people stared at me because of the rashes and bleeding, broken skin. She explained the whole thing to me."

Lexi was relieved, but more worried. She began to tear, and the waterfall began. She couldn't stop. Gus pulled her close again and tried to comfort her. After several moments of uncontrollable sobbing, she finally regained her composure.

"Why were you here with that asshole?" Lexi blubbered.

"You mean Eddie?"

"That son-of-a-bitch you were with this morning."

Gus was confused. "How do you know him?"

Lexi wasn't sure if she should tell him, but he needed to know in case 'Eddie' had much to do with him.

"When I left you that morning, he followed me all day. Then when I had to stop at a rest site, he caught me and raped me. He left me for dead."

Gus sucked in air. The happiness that had flooded him was jerked away in a few words. Rage filled him. *That's why he has kept in touch; he wanted to know about Lexi.*

Gus's face was flushed and strained. He stood up and walked a short way from Lexi. He used his cell phone to dial Metro. Breathing irregularly, he said, "This is Officer Gus Ferguson. I'd like to speak to the Watch Commander." He ordered reports on Eddie DeLuca, and he wanted a printout by the time he got to the office. He wondered *if he really is a cop—all that interest in the mobster on the hill. How could I have been so stupid to think a guy like Eddie would really be interested in my life?*

The concerned father walked slowly back to Lexi. Trying to control his rage against Eddie and the drive to see his son, he said, "Are the tests over for Awi?"

"Yes. We just have to hear the results, but given the circumstances and Scooter's anger with Eddie, we probably will head for home as soon as you and I are finished here; the results can be mailed." She was thinking, *I've got to get her out of here before she kills Eddie.*

"Can I see Awi?"

"Of course, you can see him." She called her sister on her cell and asked her to bring the baby to the lobby.

The young woman approached the parents slowly. She handed the baby to Lexi and a walked away a distance to give them private time.

Lexi presented Gus his son. "Gus meet Awi."

Red faced, the Irishman accepted his little boy gingerly as though he were receiving a fragile gift. He didn't really know how to hold a baby, and Awi was wiggling; he was tired of being confined and probed.

"Hello, Awi. It's very nice to meet you." Gus couldn't believe his eyes. He said, "He's a mini me!" Tears welled in his eyes as they met Lexi's and their arms encircled their new family.

From a distance, Scooter witnessed them; she had the same eerie feeling she had when she thought she saw a teepee near the mountain the night Awi was born. It was curious and she couldn't pin it down for a minute. She didn't have to go very far to figure it out; it was right there in front of her. This was the spirit of family love and protection. It was the same as the spirit from their ancestors that had been there the night Awi was born to protect him when they warned her and left the dark mark on Awi's forehead to signify they were watching. *It's the same warning of danger so that asshole must be close.*

Gus, emotional and barely audible, whispered, "I have to be able to find you; I need an address and phone number."

"I'm not sure if I can. I need to talk to Scooter." She tried to walk away from Gus with the dumbfounded look on his face, but he stopped her.

Control had returned to his voice. "Why do you have to talk to your sister? Awi is our son and I need to know where I can find him."

Lexi knew he had a point, but she wasn't sure if Scooter wanted him to know where they lived. She said, "We live with Scooter and to give out her information might not be agreeable with her."

***

Eddie DeLuca's mind had been churning since he saw the twins. His main reason for marrying was to give his father an heir because that's what the old man wanted. And that morning he had seen him. *I know that baby has to be mine. Gus isn't enough of a man to father a child.* Now his wife had lost the one she was carrying, so his plan was to replace that one with his own.

After taking his wife to the hotel that afternoon, he went back to the hospital. He arrived in time to witness the scene with the baby. He watched as the unscarred twin backed away to let the three get to know one another. His desire for her body was slowing down his thought process. *Down boy. You'll have her soon.*

Eddie approached the front desk of the hospital. He flashed his badge and asked to see the security officer on duty. The desk attendant pointed him in the right direction.

Eddie introduced himself to the officer and explained that he had been in the emergency room with his wife the last several hours, and they had overheard the staff discussing beautiful twins with a sick baby. His wife had just lost his baby, so they were especially open to their pain. He understood that they had problems and he and his wife wanted to help out. He wondered if the officer could help him find out their names and an address where he could reach them.

It so happened that in their discussion, Eddie and the security officer found out they were both from Chicago and had a lot in common. They visited while the officer used the computer to track down the information Eddie needed. He thanked the officer and they agreed to see one another for dinner the next time he was in town.

XIX

Scooter had noticed Eddie coming in the front of the hospital while Gus and Lexi were bonding with their son. She watched for a minute and slipped away in the direction Eddie had walked.

Eddie couldn't help notice Scooter following him and didn't try to evade her. Once she had his attention, she walked down the stairs to the basement of the hospital. The light seemed muted and hazy even with the fluorescent tubes burning. She knew he would be there soon. She thought, *this is weird. I'm not scared. Every time I have something in mind for a puke, I should be afraid, but I never have been except maybe for that time with the idiots, and that wasn't for me; it was for Lex and Awi.*

Footsteps were soft and carefully placed. Scooter leaned forward out of the dark corner she had picked. Eddie saw her and said, "There you are, you little fox. I knew you wanted me when you shoved me up against the wall."

Scooter waited for him with her nitrile gloved hands behind her. A few moments and he stood right in front of her. She raised her face to smile into his, and almost touching his chest, she moved her hands up his arms and squeezed him gently at first, then raised her knee hard into his groin. Groaning as he doubled over, he was able to slam her to the concrete floor. He reached for her, leaning forward to deliver a knockout blow to her face the way he had to Lexi, but was met by a strong elbow to the base of his nose as Scooter regained her feet. He floundered backward, lost his footing, and fell on his butt. He was stunned when his head hit the cement.

The young woman drew the blade from her boot. She landed on Eddie full force with both knees on his chest, and kept her eyes on his dazed ones while she held the knife to his throat. She unzipped his pants quickly with the other hand, found the shrunken worm, turned her attention to it for a second, and quickly sliced it off. She carefully laid the knife snug against his throat, held it there with her knee, and closed his nostrils with one hand, while the maggot found its resting place in his open mouth almost shoved down his throat.

Whispering close to his ear, Scooter said, "Hey, Son-of-a-Bitch. If I ever see you again, I will legalize you properly because if anybody ever needed killin', it's you." She thought, *I didn't have enough time to properly prepare this time. Actually, I didn't have time with the idiots, either. It's much easier without the ceremony.* Walking slowly away, she removed her gloves, peeling them off her hands and putting them in her pocket for disposal later. She turned for another look. He was gasping and trying to sit up. He pulled his precious part from his mouth, realization hit him, and he began to scream.

The entire scene lasted less than a minute, but already the blood was beginning to drain away from his buttocks.

***

Gus, Lexi, and Awi were still visiting as Scooter returned from her adventure. She had stopped by the restroom to check her appearance. Timing and previous experience had kept her out of the blood trail and as far as she could tell, she had completed her mission unscathed.

Security personnel were reacting to some disturbance in the basement as the new family left the hospital. Scooter had told Gus that he was welcome at the fort, but that he was not to share the location with anyone, ever.

Gus and Lexi needed time together, but Scooter insisted that they get home. They all went back to the room across from the hospital. Missie Wyya was suspicious of Gus, but soon understood that he was welcome. A short time later with their things packed in the Jeep, the new dad had to relinquish his loved ones. He had another task to check on.

The Jeep was pointed towards Oklahoma and Gus was headed for his office. There were two folders on his desk. Eddie DeLuca had been found in the basement of the hospital with his penis severed, and he was in surgery. Noticing the time, Gus thought, *that's about the time I was there.*   The Watch Commander had followed his directions and had given him all the information available on Eddie.

Gus was livid and had no compassion for someone who would rape; *not to mention, he raped the woman I love.* The report was several pages. The Chicago police officer had attended expensive schools, so Gus knew he had money behind him. He traced his background that led to the leader of the mob family in Illinois. Gus wondered why no one had ever checked on him before, and he realized that there would have been no reason if he'd never been implicated in a crime. *He probably had everything else covered up.*

Gus spoke to his supervisor and was given the investigation on DeLuca; it wasn't murder, but he already had so much information on Eddie. When he arrived at the hospital, he checked with security and was led to the basement crime scene. He photographed the area, drew his sketch, and took samples of the blood. The area was clean for a basement. He gave the cleaning crew the go ahead.

He was able to find the room Eddie would be moved into once he was out of surgery. There were two men dressed in expensive suits sitting just outside the room. Gus introduced himself as a fellow officer and friend and told them he had spent the last evening with Eddie and his wife, and he was concerned about his condition.

The men appeared to be very cautious and did not identify themselves. One asked him if he knew anything about what happened, and Gus offered that he had heard about the incident at dispatch.

Gus walked back to the lobby to ask questions. He learned that Eddie had asked about security, so Gus questioned the guard on duty. The young officer told him the man in the photo Gus showed him had asked for information on twins with a baby. Their address was of most importance and because he was a police officer and fellow Chicagoan, he gave him the post office address.

While Gus was talking to security, a limo pulled up out front. The well dressed driver opened the door for six men dressed like the two by Eddie's room except that they each had earpieces that reminded Gus of FBI communications.

Carefully stepping with a walking stick, an older gentleman with snow white hair entered the hospital. Eddie's wife seemed to appear out of nowhere to embrace the man. Gus recognized the man as the well known senator from Illinois.

XX

The surgery lasted for hours; reattaching a penis is a delicate business. It can be done, but the rehabilitation to help it recover its expertise is long and time consuming.

In the recovery room, Eddie was sedated, but still angry. His arms were thrashing in slow motion and fighting the many intrusive tubes and anyone who came close to him. Even in slow motion, his wife received a fist to the jaw as she moved too close to him. A scream escaped as she hit the floor. She thought, *you pig. You deserved this!*

Unfortunately for him, his father-in-law was just outside the room and witnessed the scene through the glass barrier. His daughter was weak from the miscarriage already; then to be abused by her husband just didn't set right with him. He called to his attendants that they were leaving and taking his daughter with him.

Eddie's father and his men had entered the area in time to witness the scene. The politician had come to comfort his daughter, and now saw what she really needed was relief from Eddie himself.

Jennifer's father gave a look to Claudio, one of the old man's men who had been cleared with intelligence to keep an eye on the senator. Claudio had enjoyed being a part of the illegal dealings with his real boss, but spending time in the political arena and being respected as a protector of one of the country's highest regarded politicians was a real turn on. He had fallen for the position and had watched Jennifer and Eddie for a long time. The son of his former chief was an ass. The many women in and out of his life were tiring even to observe. For someone like Eddie to have such a wonderful wife and screw around like a mad dog made Claudio judgmental; *I'd like to pop him myself.*

A look of permission given by the snow haired man, moved Claudio into action. He was in the room and had Jennifer in his arms in a minute. She was light as a feather for his muscular frame. Jennifer, with her head on his shoulder, roused and looked into Claudio's unmasked eyes; she knew she was safe.

The senator acknowledged the mob master with a nod only as he ushered his daughter and Claudio out. The politician didn't want anyone to connect them outside of the family obligations because their children were married. The old man and his sharply dressed protectors stepped back and gave them plenty of room. The old man gave a warning look to Claudio.

***

The next day, Eddie was coming out of the anesthesia. The nurses learned a new vocabulary. He demanded more pain killers and cussed anyone who would not do what he wanted. He wanted only male nurses because he thought he'd kill any woman that got close to his private parts. The old man came to see him and told him straight out to act like a human being and not the idiot he knew he was.

Ordinarily, Eddie would have talked back to him and told him to back off, but he actually needed some help and didn't want to fight with him.

"Hey, Pop. I need your help."

The weary head of crime in Chicago said, "You need my help. I'll be a son-of-a-bitch! I've never heard you say that before. I guess cutting off part of your manhood slowed you a bit. What is it?"

"You know that woman I told you I killed—the one that murdered your nephews? Well, she didn't die. I did everything I could to her except cut her throat, and I was sure she was dead. Anyway, I raped her more than once that night, and she has a baby. Since Jennifer lost the baby, and I know how much you want a grandchild, I thought I'd take that one." He hurried on so as not to lose his father's attention and his own nerve. "I got their post office box information from security here at the hospital and I know one of the staff at my office can find the street address. Then the boys and I can go get your grandson."

There it was. In his lucid moments, Eddie had thought of nothing else since he had seen the baby and since Cyanna had shoved him up against the wall. He had never talked to the old man this way before, and he had begun to be proud of himself.

The ruler of his faction stated emphatically, "You ARE an idiot. I can't say it any other way. I'm thinking that there are no words to say how stupid that whole idea is. If your mother were here today, I'd shoot her in the head for ever getting me in the sack to make such an idiot. " He threw up his hands in exasperation.

"But, Pop. You have told me so many times that you want a grandchild from me."

Trying to settle himself, he took a deep breath. "I didn't necessarily want a child from you. I wanted a child from Jennifer and you so I could have leverage over her dad and his whole family of politicians. I never told you, but I thought you were smart enough to figure that out. Evidently, NOT. What was I thinking?" (He smacked himself in the head with the palm of his hand.) "You are a FUCKIN' Idiot!" He stalked out of the room.

Eddie was not discouraged. He knew his plan had a few problems, but he could still do it. But if the old man didn't want the kid, what was the point. He knew. *That Bitch! She needs to be shown what's what. She's going to pay.*

The old man and his group left the hospital for home that day.

XXI

Cyanna, Lexi, Awi, and Missie Wyya arrived home in only a couple of days driving. The twins had taken turns driving like they had when they first went to have Awi's testing. They were delighted to be in a secure environment.

The fort was exactly as they had left it; nothing was even dusty. Missie Wyya checked her property in the confines of the compound. As the girls were watching her, Scooter said, "You know we need to find her a mate. We need to expand our pack."

Before Awi had become so ill, there had been the plans for the Pow Wow and through making the plans, the girls had contacted a tribe in South Dakota who had wolves. They back tracked and found the information. When they called the chief, he offered to meet with them to introduce his pack and his tribal family.

A road trip now when they had just come home did not seem to be a good idea, mainly because Awi was still not well, and they didn't have the results of his testing. But the fact still remained that Missie Wyya needed a mate. Scooter wasn't going anyplace without her family, so they decided to invite the chief and his entourage to their home. They had plenty of room in the fort for them to have rooms and in the compound for teepees and the wolves.

The chief agreed to make the trip. He brought four of his finest unmated wolves, his sons, their families, and the tribe Shaman with him. They set up their teepees in the compound in front of the trees, even though Scooter had offered the chief the guest room. The wolves introduced themselves. Missie Wyya was protective of her territory to begin with, but later relaxed, once she saw the rest of her family getting to know them.

Scooter talked to the Shaman every morning before the families were up and around. She explained her concern over Awi Usdi and asked him for direction. He told her that the way of the modern man is good, but the old ways are always more effective. He volunteered to give the child a healing ceremony that he had given many times in his long life. He explained that the important part of the ritual is to balance Awi within himself. Scooter thought, *maybe that's why I keep balancing myself with those who make my world out of balance.* She smiled.

Scooter accompanied the Native Americans who traveled to the nearby reservation. The Shaman collected herbs for the ceremony while she attended their social gatherings and invited them to take part in the Pow Wow for Awi's first birthday that would be held after a ceremony for his health.

The next evening, one of the teepees was cleared of everything except a heavy bear rug off to the side of the central fire area. There was room for the family, including Missie Wyya. Awi was the guest of honor. The other visiting guests were chanting softly outside holding hands to make a circle around the teepee.

The older Native American chanted his song to the little boy lying on the furry rug, set his rattle down, and gave Awi a sip from a potion made up of the herbs he had obtained from the reservation visit. He continued softly and gave Awi another sip. The ritual continued for more than an hour.

Lexi, Scooter, and Missie Wyya were watching very carefully. The light from the fire accompanied by the soft song calmed the family and Awi. The little boy did not wake up that night after the ceremony; he slept until morning. Time passed without incident as Awi regained his strength and learned to walk.

The plans were made for the Pow Wow, the South Dakota tribe stayed, the locals came, and the wolves played like children together. The Pow Wow was different from the last one the girls had together—no Gram, no memorial to their mother, no mysterious teepee. The focus on new life and new family was the theme. Gus was invited. There were the dancers and music, the different tribal groups, the great food with deep pit beef and pork, and merriment deep into the night.

Gus began to understand the connection between the twins and their devotion to family. He watched as Missie Wyya attended Awi and took every step he took and because he was new at the process, he held onto the wolf's fur to steady himself. The new father watched the twins take part in the dances and noted how much they looked like they belonged in their ceremonial gowns.

The officer couldn't be absent from his job for more than a month, but during that time he learned to be a part of the Ahwi family. Awi looked for him every morning and tried to walk or crawled over to him whenever he entered the room.

The time came for the chief to take his family back to their home. Scooter was sorry to see them go and was indebted to him for bringing Missie Wyya an acceptable mate. She tried to pay him, but he pointed out that they were now connected by the spirit of the wolf.

Lexi and Gus found one another and bonded as though they had never been apart. When the officer's vacation time was over, he could not bear to leave his new family. He knew he must speak to Lexi about their future.

"Lexi, I don't want to leave you or Awi. I've been thinking about this for a while; I'm going to take early retirement. I need to know if this would work with my coming here to be with you; I know you don't want to live where I live because of what happened before."

"Gus, you know I love you, and I would like you to be a part of our lives. We need to talk to Scooter and see what she thinks." Gus was concerned about the outcome of such a conversation.

Gus and Lexi walked out to Scooter in the compound. The weather had been warm for a few weeks, but the evenings were still nice. Missie Wyya and her new beau, Kanati were expecting puppies within a few weeks and still seemed to enjoy one another's company. Both wolves catered to Awi who was trying out faster walking which made him fall. He wasn't dismayed; he'd get up and try again, giggling all the way.

"Sis, Gus and I want to talk to you about something."

"Shoot."

Gus began, "The last few weeks have been more than I could have hoped for. I love Lexi and Awi and I don't want to leave them. I wouldn't want to impose and I'd pay my own way. I'll have a good retirement. How would you feel about my coming here to live?"

Scooter was quiet for a few minutes as she gazed at the forest at the base of the shear mountain that was the back of the compound. *I love it here.*

"Well, I'll tell you. When Lex wanted to tell you about Awi, I was against it, but now I think I was wrong. It turns out that finding you was good for Awi not only because of the family information you had to offer, especially with the recent test results confirming what you have told us, but you are a genuine and have a good soul. I know Lexi loves you, and Awi thinks you are his own private property. Wyya and Kanati like you, so you can't be all bad. Welcome to our pack."

Gus and Lexi breathed a sigh of relief. Joy indescribable washed over them. They were to be a family or pack as Scooter said. Gus circled his arm around Lexi's waist and they stood for a long while watching their son play with the wolves.

XXII

The therapy Eddie had to endure every day to train his reconnected penis to drain made him more determined to make Scooter pay for what she had done to him. The day came for him to see if his reattached member would function the way he had used it for so many years.

Jennifer had stood by him and his nastiness during his recovery. She had been a good wife in the beginning of their marriage before she realized who he really was, but had planned to divorce him once he was well.

One evening as they were preparing for bed, Eddie approached Jennifer and tried to kiss her. She evaded his embrace and pulled away. He grabbed her by the arm and said, "I need to know if this thing will work."

"Why don't you try it out on one of your working girls?"

Unashamed, Eddie said, "If it doesn't work, I don't want to be embarrassed."

"Thanks, a lot, Asshole!" Eddie slapped her hard across the face.

"I need to make a baby with you for Pop." The humiliation ignited the realization that the reason for their marriage was a baby to connect the families.

"I'll never have a baby of yours! I've had three abortions!" She thought, *maybe that's why I lost the last one that I didn't want to lose.* "Now that you are up and running, I'm leaving your sorry ass!"

Eddie chased her out of the house. Jennifer had known this was coming and had planned her escape for a while. She was in her car and on her way to Claudio before the surprised jerk could call his guards.

The next morning Eddie called the precinct and asked for the street address connected to the post office box he had gotten from the hospital security officer. It didn't take long and he had the address. He thought, *Oklahoma! Why in Hell would anyone want to live in Oklahoma?*

The young mobster called his men together and laid out the plan he was about to initiate. He gave strict instructions that the twin without the scar was his and to bring her to him once they got into the house and found her. Anybody else they could kill.

***

Scooter, Lexi, Awi, Gus, Missie Wyya, Kanati, and the puppies were a close family. Gus had retired and vowed to pay his share of expenses. He had never had the feeling of belonging like he had with his new family. He was part of them and didn't try to impose his will in any way.

Gus had become more than an asset with his carpentry skills. Any repairs around the compound were taken care of as soon as he was aware of them. He was pleasant and accommodating. Love was the key; they were a pack.

The day dawned clear and pristine. There was no wind, and there was calm within the group. About dusk the family was out observing the wolves and Awi playing in the back yard near the stand of trees. Missie Wyya stopped in her tracks; she alerted to some faint something and the hair stood up on her back just behind her neck. Kanati heard it, too. Scooter took one look at the wolves and turned to see the dust rolling behind what seemed to be a procession of vehicles coming toward the fort.

Scooter shouted for Gus and Lexi to get into the house as she ran for Awi. She scooped him up with the wolves following. Gus and Lexi were right behind her. The train of black SUVs drove through the chain link fence and slid to a stop just in front of the fortress. The last pup scurried inside, the door slammed, and Scooter reached for the electronic panel to lock down the house. The steel shutters closed as the doors locked.

Awi was squealing; he thought they were playing. The puppies were not so sure, and Missie Wyya and Kanati were on alert and growling. Scooter checked through the lookout and realized there were four SUVs and she counted seven men. She turned to Lexi and ordered, "Lex, take Awi and the pups and go to the basement. There is a panel on the wall. Push the green button to open the door; when you are loaded and in the Jeep on the other side, push the button to close it. Gus you go with her; Awi needs you both. Everything you need is in the Jeep."

In a high pitched voice, "I can't leave you." Lexi began to cry.

Gus asked, "What are you talking about?"

Scooter enlightened him. "Gus because of what happened to us last time, I prepared for this possibility. There are seven men outside and they didn't come to visit. Take a look."

Gus looked out to see men armed with machine guns. His grey hair went static very like the wolves hair on the back of their necks.

"Lex, we don't have time to argue. Go, take the babies. You have minutes before all Hell breaks loose."

Lexi turned to Scooter, "I can't lose you again."

Scooter said simply as their eyes met and she tapped her chest with her fingers, "I will always be with you. Now, go."

Scooter pulled out her grandfather's .45 and began to load it. Gus noticed the round steel ball that she added. He started to protest and insist that he was going to stay and help. Scooter commanded, "**GO**." He could see in her eyes there was no room for discussion. After taking Awi from Lexi, he hurriedly followed her and the puppies to the basement.

Seconds later, the bullets began to fly. Lexi found the control panel at the bottom of the stairs and pushed the button. The automatic door slid somewhere overhead to reveal a fully equipped Jeep complete with cage in the back for the puppies. Awi was quickly strapped in his baby seat, the puppies were locked in the cage, and Lexi, tears streaming down her face, pushed the button on the exit side, and started the engine. She had difficulty following the tunnel out the back of the complex. She had known about the escape route but had expected Scooter to be with her, so she hadn't paid much attention to the surroundings. The noise from the machine guns spurred her on.

Scooter was re-loading her rifles in the hidden cabinets and picking off the intruders, one at a time, through the shooting channels in the doors. The walls were holding and slowing down the bullets much better than they had at Gram's house. She was able to move from one area of arms and ammunition to another without much deterrent. The invaders were trying to kick in the steel doors without success. The wolves were ready if any made it through.

Lexi and Gus could still hear the bullet barrage. She understood what she needed to do. To lose Awi or Gus would destroy her. To be without her sister would leave a big hole in her heart. She focused and the Jeep made it out of the tunnel undetected by the would-be murderers.

Eddie had had enough. He hadn't participated in the actual shooting or trying to kick in the doors. A radio talk station he enjoyed was playing and he didn't want to miss any of it. But these clowns were taking too long. He could see no one still moving. He backed up the SUV a distance and drove forward as fast as the distance would allow. The vehicle exploded through the front door leaving mangled steel and vehicle parts like torn tissue in an open wound.

Eddie tried to pull himself out of the air bag, but it was too late. Missie Wyya had an arm and Kenati had a leg. Scooter had him in a death grip and pulled him out by his neck. Dazed again, she dropped him on his knees and walked around in front of him. He gazed upward into her cold, steady eyes.

Scooter was trembling inside, not from fear, but from fury and the very idea one person could take it upon themselves to dictate the future of another's life. Rape destroys the emotional being within a soul. He had hurt her twin as only a depraved person could. She was deliberate and did not hesitate.

***

Gus and Lexi had found their way out of the tunnel; she hadn't noticed the brush and tree branches covering of the exit, but they crashed through it to a dirt road, anyway. They made it to the nearby town and brought the police back to the fortress within an hour.

Lexi ran toward the fort opening with Gus right behind her. Lights from the police cruisers showed the bodies of the attackers around the perimeter of the house, and inside they found Eddie still on his knees with his back leaning up against the wreckage of his SUV. While the couple stared at him, an officer accidently bumped the side of the vehicle while turning his attention to another corner of the room, and Eddie's head rolled off the body to the floor.

As he watched the head roll to a stop, Gus realized that Eddie's and Castanzo's brutal deaths along with the round bullet from the Castanzo killing and the .45 Scooter had loaded a few hours before very well could connect the murders and Scooter. There would have to be extensive testing, but that wasn't his job anymore. His realization was that he had not included the twins in any of his final reports, except to point out they were not found, so to connect this mess with the other one would be impossible. He would not have pursued it anyway because the puke who had tried to destroy his pack had met his justified end.

Lexi was relieved they hadn't found her sister or the wolves. She knew they were somewhere together because she could feel the peace. She also knew that wherever Scooter was, she had been true to her word. She wouldn't have to tell her about Eddie, and she had a strange sense of relief that he wouldn't be raping anyone else.

***

A few months later, Gus, Lexi, and Awi attended a Pow Wow near the fortress they had rebuilt; they were introducing Awi to his heritage. A dance, a new dance, Lexi had not seen before was being performed. It was the story of a young warrior running with wolves on either side as in a pack.

A trickle of nerve synapses traveled up Lexi's spine ending with tears in her eyes. She knew someone in the local tribe had seen Scooter and the wolves leaving that night after the break in; this was the first proof of the peace within her.